The Origami

Theory

The Origami

Theory

By
Raynesha Pittman and Niles Manning

Conglomerate Ink, PO BOX 512 Shelbyville, TN 37162

Editing by: Joy Hammond Nelson

Cover Design by: Mario Patterson

ISBN13: 978-06785617

ISBN10: 0996785612

# Dedication

This is dedicated to Sadako Sasaki, the 12-year-old Japanese girl who died chasing The Origami Theory. At the tender age of two, an age where most of us are protected from the evils of the world, Sadako suffered from radiation poison when an atomic bomb was dropped on Hiroshima, Japan.

Growing up with the illness, and seeing the post effects of a world terrified by nuclear warfare, she still dared to dream, she dared to have Hope. She heard of the Chinese Legend where if you fold a thousand paper cranes you would be granted a wish. As a sick child watching her own life deteriorate beneath her feeble eyes, she pursued this goal of a thousand cranes. The most important part about her story is that her wish wasn't for health, for strength, or to be ridden from the toxin that was threatening her life, she only had one wish...World Peace.

Sadly, she died before she could finish the cranes, and here we are. Still today you can find people on the street chasing that theory in hopes of a wish whatever it may be. Drug dealers stack bloody money, covered in the radiation of dope just to one day have enough to make a wish and escape the lifestyle that they are currently in. Strippers poison their self-esteem for the crinkled likes of one dollar bills, in hopes that someone throws enough to one day make something beautiful out of it. Whether you trade stocks, steal cars for 10% of the value, or shine shoes outside of a Washington, D.C. pub, we all are chasing a wish.

So, we take that back, this isn't dedicated to Sadako, because in a twisted notion she got her wish, she finally has peace...within. No, we dedicate this one to you, the person reading this. What will you make beautiful out of your money?

# Loyal Folds

A single lavender candle burned in the far corner of the room. The flame was on its last ignition as the wax thinned beneath it, revealing the glass bottom of the jar. On its final hoorah, the flame illuminated the small bedroom of the condo, casting an enormous shadow of the burly figure on the bed. The ceiling fan was on low, barely cycling a draft as beads of sweat cascaded down the rolls of a flaccid middle-aged back. He wiped his slick head and flung trickles of perspiration across the room, landing on the thin fabric of the drapes. A small pool formed and leaked down onto the floor, where his size 44" jeans were crumbled up under the window.

Big Unc, Unc, Uncle, or whatever you felt the desire to call him, had gripped the reigns of Rock City's underworld for decades. He started out thumping heroin in the 70's, under the leadership of his stepdad, a smooth character with the persona of a pimp, and the malice of a hitman. From the moment his mother introduced him to Sylvester, aka Silk, Big Unc idolized his character. He watched as Silk took his mother, a once proud independent woman of class, and molded her from a soft-spoken square, to a sharp edged, short skirt wearing, high pumps balancing, diva. He molded her like clay in the lap of a sculptor, Play-Doh in the palm of a child, or if she was plaster under the trowel of a carpenter. If any man had the power to replace God in God-fearing Denise, then Big Unc wanted to try on his snakeskin shoes.

Decades later, with Silk and Denise both deteriorating into ashes in parallel graves, from an unsolved double murder; Big Unc was still carrying the torch…a flame that would never subside.

The candle died in the corner of the room…

"Stop running from this dick! You called me over here, right?" Big Unc asked as he clasped the female's waist with his large hands. He slammed her cheeks back against his thighs and hanging gut as she released a seductive moan, fueling his eternal flame like wax. She looked back at him and bit down on her bottom lip. The light from the adjacent building shined through the window, adding soft amber to their chocolate bodies. "Be careful what you ask for!" Big Unc said as he thrust deeper inside of her- a deeper love inside his militant heart, and she was his Sister Souljah.

No Disrespect though…

Respectfully, at 350lbs, he was a bully in the sheets. He ruled his lustful playground with an iron dick, especially after popping half of a Viagra before the bell rang. He swung from woman to woman, and they hung onto his words and rusty promises like monkey bars. He would slide down their love canal, cheer, and then run back up it just for the sport...just to conquer. It was nothing for him to whisper sweet nothings, meaningless nothings, and have their heads spinning like merry-go-rounds. It was sickening. Some got dizzy and even puked from premeditated morning sickness. It was a hard pill to swallow the morning after.

The stronger students of the game stood back and watched as he took advantage of the weaker souls. Whatever he saw...he saw. He'd hold them up on his wood, allowing them to think that they were on top, and then he'd drop them to Earth, as he stood up- dismantling their trust. He hopped from box to box like hopscotch- one foot in and another already out the door. Being a bully was his only hobby, and he balanced it well.

The victim in front of him was no different. He pushed her down and pulled her ass up, arching her back. She tried to prop herself up but he smacked her arms from under her like the new kid's tray in the cafeteria. He grabbed her ass cheeks and pinched them, even though her thong was green. With drunken eyes dilated with lust, he leaned over, and pulled her undergarment to the side, revealing her pink lips. He flicked them. He kissed them, as his dick got even harder from her moans. He could feel the shivers trembling through her body as his warm tongue flirtatiously teased her. She was enjoying his bullying at the moment.

"Let me put it in your ass," she heard him say. Her eyes shot open as she looked back. Her plush cheeks obstructed her view as he pestered her even more. Maybe if she ignored the request, he'd forget about it.

"That wasn't a request..." Big Unc licked his finger and gave her rectum a Wet Willy. Then he rose up and jammed his wet Willie where his finger was- she clenched like a Chinese finger trap. She tried to escape as she screamed, but he pulled her back by the integrity of her thong. He yanked on it like he was at a rodeo- merely horseplay, giving her the worst wedgie imaginable. She pleaded as he shoved his dick further into her ass, but her cries only amused his intoxicated state. He reached forward and pulled her hair...because that's how little boys flirt...

Reece sat in a folding chair in the hallway as he waited on his boss and kept a watchful eye. Big Unc was reckless, but cautious with the same hand. He never went anywhere alone, and as his advisor, Reece always seemed to be sitting on the other side of the door during one of Big Unc's rendezvous...it was like déjà vu, a taboo practice for what he originally signed up for.

As he swiped through his phone, trying his best to ignore the screams of the poor girl and the chants of his mentor, Reece reflected on how he got where he was. Big Unc always had a strong presence in his youth. He practically financed the local Boys & Girls club when the city threatened to close that chapter due to budgeting. He was deeply involved in Rock City High's sports program, even though his interest was in finding a future star early enough to cash out on in the future; his public intentions were honorable. Everyone respected him, and ignored where the money came from, even parents of the children- that's how Reece came to be where he was.

Big Unc took Reece under his arm early when he saw the kid selling mixed cd's in front of a corner store. Reece was a hustler, even at an early age, and showed signs of a potential businessman. His little tent had everything from music, to cologne, to tall tees, and even audio systems for cars. Most of his merchandise was stolen, but that's what attracted Big Unc; Reece had a knack for turning dirty money into clean bills. That inspired Big Unc to scoop him up off of the streets before the asphalt claimed him and sent him to school. Reece's education was paid for with drug money, and now he was laundering it back into the hands of Big Unc by bringing his knowledge and advice to the organization.

Reece looked up as Big Unc stepped out of the bedroom buckling his jeans. His stomach hung over his waistline like a pot boiling over, a compliment to his sweaty skin. A silk shirt was draped over his bare shoulder, resembling a wrestler exiting the cage. He stared at Reece with low eyelids as he stuffed his arms into his shirt and buttoned it up to the best of his abilities.

"Recess over?" Reece asked as he stood to his feet. Big Unc grinned and stepped past him. They exited the condo and immediately the night air attacked Big Unc's damp flesh. He shuffled over to the rear of the Cadillac XTS and slid across the plush leather interior. Reece hopped in the driver's seat and started up the automobile. He wasn't the driver on paper, but during Unc's most secretive escapades, he was enlisted for the task.

"Wife called?" Unc asked. Reece bent his arm back and handing him his cellphone.

"Yup. Three times." Unc checked the device and leaned back with a deep sigh. He started examining himself for evidence of his infidelity...the ol' lipstick on the collar bit. "Brass called as well. That I answered," Reece said as he glanced up into the rearview mirror. Unc had already dug into his stash and retrieved a pint of Hennessy Black. He turned the bottle up to his lips and wiped the excess from his graying goatee.

"What did Brass want?" Unc asked as he closed his red eyes like late flights and relaxed.

"He said it was classified. Had to be said in person."

Unc rolled his eyes and took another swig. "Classified…probably dealing with that nigga D-Rock."

"I'm guessing," Reece said as he waited at the stoplight. "You want me to swing you by his spot real quick?" Unc fanned his hand.

"Nah, I can't deal with that shit right now. You go. That's what I pay you for. I gotta get home before this lady kills me."

"I'm your advisor, Unc," Reece reminded him. "Plus, since we are on the subject, I still have that proposition that I want to talk you about." Unc blew his lips in frustration. "Unc, you brought me on board to help, and that's what I'm trying to do. Now I have a few ventures that-" Reece looked into the mirror and saw Unc holding his palm forward, stopping him midsentence.

"My head already throbs. Please, let's not talk business right now, ok Reece?"

"You got it, boss…" he answered sarcastically. Unc hated when he called him that and Reece knew it. He didn't view Reece as a brainless worker, but as his son. He created the business-minded soldier that sat before him, so he couldn't rightfully be angered at his ambition, but now wasn't the time.

"I know you want to go legit, but that transition isn't as easy as you think, kiddo," Unc commented as he stared out the window.

"Nor is it as hard as you think…but we'll talk, Unc. I'ma convince you sure enough," Reece said as he nodded. Truth be told, he didn't have a plan at the moment, but he knew that drug money didn't last forever. They needed a business to launder the blood money and keep the feds off their scent. With everything that was going haywire in the streets, it was only a matter of time before RICO came swooping in.

Reece turned down a dark path that led up to Unc's manor. It was a beautiful estate, acres on acres of picturesque lawn with Greek statues scattered about like the graveyard of Mount Olympus. A stone driveway wrapped around the front meadow, circling a sculpture of cupid with a fountain sprouting from his hands. His traditional bow and arrow lie at his feet, embedded into the stone.

Reece stopped the car in front of the immaculate home and looked at Unc in the mirror. He was passed out. Reece hated dealing with drunks, and he dreaded it even more when they weighed nearly 350lbs. Luckily, that blob of alcohol paid his ugly salary…handsomely.

Reece opened the backdoor and pulled at Unc's arm. He woke up a bit and stepped out of the vehicle, enough for Reece to wrap his arm over his shoulder and escort him towards the steps. Reece looked up and saw DeAndrea standing at the door in an all-black nightgown. Her caramel skin shined through the cloth as she crossed her arms to cover her perky nipples from the draft. She shook her head as Reece virtually carried Unc to the door.

"A damn shame…" The sound of his wife's voice was like ammonia capsules under Unc's nostrils. He looked up and tried his best to regain his composure and balance.

"Thanks, Reece," he said as he patted him on the back without even looking at him. "Go meet with Brass and handle that situation." He leaned in to kiss DeAndrea on her cheek, but nearly lost his footing. He had to grab the door to save face.

"You smell like cheap perfume and latex," DeAndrea said as she shook her head. Unc pretended as if he didn't hear her and disappeared into the house. She focused her attention on Reece who was still standing at the top of the steps looking foolish. He could read her eyes and fired off an excuse for his boss.

"We were at a strip club. He had a little too much to drink, D. Nothing happened though," Reece said with a smile.

"You dare stand there and say that dumb shit to me?" Reece's smile leveled out as the seriousness of her voice stabbed the air. She stepped closer and dropped her arms, revealing her gumdrop nipples that pitched tents under her gown; the campfire in her heart for her husband was long extinguished. She fell for the kingpin out of lust, for the finer things in life. What was an image of a heavenly lifestyle, turned out to be a mirage. 15 years his junior, she was kept as a trophy wife, placed on a mantle to show off his accomplishments, while he still played the field and entertained honorable mentions...like a field day.

Reece looked away, trying not to make it so obvious that he was staring at his boss's wife; especially with him just inside. "I expect him to lie to me, not you," she said flatly. Reece gathered himself and walked back towards his car.

"I'm just his advisor, D. Whether he chooses to listen is ultimately his call," he said as he opened the door.

"Reece..." she started till she heard Unc rambling through the cupboards in the kitchen.

"Where's the fucking aspirin?" he called out. She looked back and then at Reece with puppy eyes of distress. He smiled and shut the driver's door. She stood on the porch and watched as he disappeared down the driveway. Part of her just wanted to stand outside forever, anything to keep from going inside the house and facing Unc and his bullshit.

"The aspirin, D...where the fuck is it?"

"You probably left it over that bitch's house!" DeAndrea shouted as she re-entered the house and slammed the door behind her.

*****

Reece parked on the side of the road on the outskirts of town, next to a large area of open field. In front of him was Brass leaning against the front of his decked-out Jeep Wrangler. Only their headlights shined in the dark, not even the moon dared to eavesdrop. Brass was a tall figure with a muscular physique that he loved to flaunt. He stood at 6'5", a soft skin tone, but a hard face that was permanently turned up into a scowl. He got his name from his excessive obsession with brass knuckles, a vintage weapon that he retro'd on many loose jaws around the city.

Standing next to him, a complete opposite in physique, was Wink. Wink stood at a whopping 5'6", had skin of coal, and beady eyes pressurized into diamonds. He gained his name from an uncontrollable twitch in the right side of his facial muscles that made it seem as if he was winking periodically. He was quiet, unlike Brass, obedient, and preferred letting his guns translate his silence and do the talking for him.

As Reece walked up, another figure hopped out of the back of the Jeep and stood next to Wink. Reece had never seen him before, and found it odd that Brass would bring new faces to a meeting that he deemed an emergency. "What's going on?" Reece asked leaning back against the front of his car, still eying the new character. Brass stepped forward and glanced at the back of Reece's car with a frown.

"Where is Unc?"

"He sent me on his behalf. Now what is all of this about?" Reece questioned. It was no secret that he and Brass bumped heads more than conjoined twins. It was mainly about power. Reece was Unc's right hand man, and business partner. Brass was family though, a true nephew. He had the Dunn blood and felt as if he was the rightful heir to the throne. The only problem was, he still had a soldier's mentality, and wasn't built to lead an empire. Unc knew this, and was vocal about it. His critiques only strengthened the tension between the two. They were from two different walks of life, but somehow met up at an intersection of fate and fortune.

"This is bullshit…" Brass said as he shook his head. "You're a fucking driver. Why am I even speaking to yo' bitch ass about this?" he asked as he leaned back against the Jeep and folded his arms. The new face watched the transaction of words, trying to get a feel for who was who.

"First off, nigga, I'm the advisor, and number two in this here operation," Reece held up two fingers mockingly towards Brass.

"Number two, huh?" Brass released a chuckle and shook his head. "The fuck ever. You're a lapdog, but ok…you got it, fam."

"If you two are done measuring dicks, can we get down to business?" the new face asked. He held his arms out in a filthy hoodie. Everything on him was tattered, from his dingy jeans to his leaning Timberlands that looked as if he used the construction boots for their intended purpose. He had short dreads that sung high notes that they hadn't experienced any T.L.C. in ages…he was a Scrub, a Creep, and Waterfalls of lameness, which made him so Unpretty…

"Who is this character?" Reece asked as he pointed with his thumb.

"Oh, this clown? This is Murph," Brass said as he lit up a cigarette. Wink stepped to the other side of Murph to avoid the stench of the smoke…or so it seemed. Murph stepped forward and held his fist out.

"Call me Murph, Murphy, Big Murph, or whatever, you feel me?" he said. Reece noticed how fidgety the guy was, and automatically suspected that he was using the crème of their crop.

"And why are you here?" Reece asked, ignoring the greeting. Murph stuffed his hands back in the pocket of his hoody. "Why is he here?" Reece repeated, this time aiming his question to Brass.

"That theory that we had on D-Rock, you remember that?" Brass asked before a deep exhale of smoke.

"Yeah. You felt like he was a snitch. What does this guy have to do with any of that?"

"He was his cellmate," Brass said with a sinister grin. Reece shifted his eyes over towards Murph.

"Damn right. That nigga was spilling beans like that Bush's baked beans dog."

"Bush dog?" Reece shrugged his shoulders in confusion. "The fuck is you talking about?"

"Listen, scratch that, ya dig. Just know this; he was in the joint telling any, and everybody, who would listen, that he got down with the Dunn family. Straight spilling that shit."

"And you were one of the ones who listened?" Reece asked as he stuffed his hands into his slacks.

"Hell yeah! Why? Cause I want to be down. I want that money that don't fold, ya feel me!" Murph broke out into laughter. "That money that don't fold! Believe that!" Reece stole a glance at Brass who just shook his head with a smirk. Brass could already read Reece's mind and found it amusing. Wink was standing still like a Marine sentry, with his hands in his leather jacket, just waiting on the next set of orders.

"Doesn't make sense. D-Rock got caught with a key. He doing ten, last I heard. Shit, last I heard he took his time like a man. Who are we to believe this cat who obviously has a motive?"

Murph smiled and looked back at Brass. "Who is this guy? I thought I was meeting the boss. Somebody who know about this street shit. Not some square with his polo tucked into some Docker slacks. Aye, no disrespect," Murph said as he turned back to Reece, "whoever you are, but I think I need to be talking to Unc. I need to meet the man in charge, feel me?"

"Come at me like that again, and you'll meet the man upstairs. Don't get shit twisted, whatever the fuck your name is," Reece said sharply. Murph had to straighten his face up. "This bullshit story that you trying to pitch holds no weight. I trust my people, you understand? D-Rock was solid. He's going to do that time with his head held high, and his voice low."

"Is that so?" Murph asked as he rubbed his chin. Reece was getting agitated at the newcomer questioning his authority. That was one reason why he hated when Brass tried to pull his slick shit in a public forum, because then everyone felt as if they could do it. "How about this, your boy D-Rock is out now. Got out a week before me. Said he was going to pack his shit and head to Phoenix."

Reece looked at Brass who nodded. "I thought...I thought he had ten? The fuck?"

"Let me add two and two together for you. The nigga snitched, took a deal, and now he is about to leave the state...that's if he hasn't already," Brass said as he flicked his cigarette.

"True shit. That's why y'all need a nigga like me on the roster. Everybody ain't as solid as you think. I did my time like a G." Reece ignored the stupid shit that was spattering out of Murph's mouth. The guy was an idiot, but he had valuable information. D-Rock did have family in Phoenix, and nobody had heard from him in months. Usually a soldier that was locked up would call for support or something in that likeness...facts weren't adding up.

Reece released a heavy sigh as he rubbed his face out of irritation. "His loyalty folded…" Brass commented.

"Go find that nigga and reroute his flight," Reece ordered with a scowl.

"No need to say that, like you calling shots, nigga. I was going to do that anyway. I just thought you and Unc should know." Brass grinned and walked towards the driver's side of his Jeep. He stepped up onto the lifted vehicle and held onto the roll cage before climbing in. "Oh, and what do you want to do with this clown?" Brass asked as he nodded at Murph. Murph was smiling at Reece while rubbing his hands in anticipation.

"Wink at him," Reece said.

"What?" Murph asked in a puzzled tone. He turned towards Brass but froze when he saw Wink aiming a pistol at him. Before he could even raise his hands and plead for his life, the front of his skull opened up, followed by the back, as he collapsed onto the dirt in a fetal position.

"Good money folds…" Reece said.

Cat Fighting

Steam rose from the asphalt of the parking lot like butter does when it's dropped in a heated skillet. It was hot and not the usual hot that the residents of Phoenix were accustomed to, but the "fry an egg on the sidewalk or brew a cup of tea on the porch, hot" like the talk radio meteorologist put it. He proclaimed the 120-degree temperature as the second hottest day in history, falling 2 degrees short of the 122-degree record breaker of 1990. The blazing rays of sunlight caused Yvette's naked eyes to displace images as she stared at the optical phenomenon known as a mirage, yet she wasn't impressed. The scorching heat outside of her comfy air conditioned BMW E38 was no match for sweltering heat she had within her.

The AC was on max but it did nothing to cool the rising heat of her body. Beads of sweat began to dance along the disintegrating edges of her hairline. Underneath the black and honey-blonde shabby lace front wig, a pool of sweat and gel began to form causing the hair to smell like slightly mildewed dry towels. Once the funky pool freed itself from the entrapment, it caused the wig to shift closer to her drawn on eyebrows. Her freshly glazed forehead had given her bright yellow skin the tone of a rotting banana from the brown gel she used to lay her natural hair down, but she was too angry to care about her appearance. And the longer she sat in her car staring at the entrance to her job, the more annoyed she felt.

Yvette had grown to hate everything about her job at the US Citizenship and Immigration Services Office and the reason for the hatred had just pulled up and parked next to her in a new baby powder white, two door, dark tinted Benz. It was the same CLS 550 Benz, minus the color and tint that she set as her screensaver at work, to give her all day access to drool over the vehicle she wanted but couldn't afford. She was positive that Ms. Perfect, the name she mockingly called Cydney amongst trusted coworkers, had purchased the car out of spite and not of desire. There was something about Cydney's flawless deep chocolate thick frame, her undeniable exotic beauty, and her award-winning personality that mirrored her work ethic that screamed she was faker than all the designer purses floating around Canal Street in New York, and yet she was still desired like them. She was perpetrating perfection and Yvette could no longer stomach her fraud.

Before Ms. Cydney Adore, transferred in from the New York field office, Yvette loved everything about helping immigrants gain temporary or permanent residency in the United States. Her work put her in a patriotic mindset and she'd convinced herself that she was working hand in hand with Homeland Security in the war on terrorism.

Yvette was always the first to work and last to leave due to volunteering for extra tasks to help her team but now her team was lucky if she even showed up. All the overtime she had worked over the past three years procured her with endless vacation days and paid time off, time that she wouldn't dare use before. Now she prayed she had enough PTO days left to make it through the month without touching her sick days.

Having an all-star Immigration Information Officer transfer in from the second largest foreign-born resident state seemed like a blessing when Cydney's transfer was announced, yet time proved it to be the exact opposite. The transfer didn't only cause Yvette to give up the privacy of her own huge office space for the newcomer; it also caused her a non-monetary demotion to a window agent. She went from being a caseworker with an oversized leather swivel chair and a mahogany desk, to a countertop, barstool, and the seated passer of needed forms and applications. To top the shit off with flies, Cydney seemed to be loved and cherished by her coworkers more than Yvette had ever been.

Cydney won the hearts of the office staff by displaying herself as this larger than life lover and advocate of the human race. If a client cried, Cydney would cry with them as she dried their tears. If there was a language barrier between her and a new client, she'd used her personal off the clock hours with the help of Rosetta Stone to master the language. She even took a reduction in pay to meet Phoenix's field office salary-cap and yet she still managed to gift the office weekly to reward everyone's hard work. Cydney was too perfect and Yvette was determined to find her flaws so she could broadcast them, even if the price to pay for the breaking news was the loss of her job.

"Knock, knock," Cydney said softly tapping on Yvette's car window.

Yvette tried to act like she was deep in prayer in hopes the devil in heels would walk away but to no avail. Instead, Cydney continued to wait patiently in the heat for her to come out of meditation. Taking a quick glance at the new villain in her life, she saw that Cydney was wearing a charcoal grey pantsuit despite the heat and decided to let her bake in the sun for a while.

"Hey girl, I'm sorry I didn't see you standing there in this heat. I was lost in prayer, God is so good!" Yvette said as she rolled down the window while fighting the urge to laugh.

"Yes, he is! I was excited to see that you made it here on time today. I was starting to think that 8:30 am instead of the mandatory 7:45 start time was your new schedule. It's a good thing salaried employees don't have to clock in or you'd be out of job. Any who, guess who brought donuts for her co-workers?" She was shaking the large box in Yvette's face but Yvette was blinded by the light bouncing off Cydney's diamond ring.

When did this bitch get engaged? That ho's rocking the rock of Gibraltar and I can't even get a fucking date to Applebee's, she thought.

"No thank you, I don't consume sugar in the morning and you should say no to all of those extra calories too. You know you're my girl and I got your back so I can be real with you, but baby, you're a donut away from turning that thick coke bottle shape of yours into a dented up two liter, boo. And I see somebody has gotten engaged over the weekend so you better tighten up before he asks for that fake ass diamond ring back!" she managed to say with counterfeit concern.

"Oh no, I wouldn't commit myself to anything or anyone except our clients. Nor could I wear fake jewelry. Those five for a dollar bangles you have on would turn my wrist green and black in a matter of seconds, but they're cute on you, girl. This..." she said extending her hand, "is just a little $15,000 reminder that I don't need a man for anything. You know what I mean, girlfriend? Seeing you haven't had a man since I first got here, well over a year ago. The heartbreak I watched you go through, the stress you were under, and that unhealthy weight loss assured me that I've made the right decision remaining single. Well, let me take these in while they're still hot, are you coming in?"

"I'll be in there in a second." Yvette said dryly reliving the heartbreak of being left at the altar not once, but twice.

"Alright, you still have 20 minutes to talk to God before we open the doors and welcome our foreign friends in. Don't let the clock beat you inside my love, toodles."

"Toodles," Yvette said before Cydney got out earshot. Once she watched her walk past the metal detectors inside the building, Yvette sparked up a conversation with God,

"God, I hate that bitch!"

*****

The U.S.C.I.S office was packed but that was usual and it was a blessing because it made the day go by faster. Lunchtime had finally arrived giving Cydney the break that she so desperately needed to relieve herself from the stresses that came with having a large caseload.

"Hey ladies, I'm headed to that new sub shop down the road. Do any of you want to partake in it with me, my treat?" she asked showing off all 32 of her freshly whitened teeth to the ladies working the customer service windows.

"I don't go on break for another 15 minutes baby, but thank you for inviting me," the elderly woman at the window left of Yvette said.

"No problem, Ms. Stella, write down what it is that you want and I'm still going to treat. Yvette," she said turning to face the first co-worker that welcomed her with open arms so many months ago. "How about you, my love? It's your weight loss advice that has me grabbing a sandwich over a burger." She laughed. "What can I get for you?"

"I don't want shit," Yvette said in a voice that sounded more like after five lingo than business professional. "I packed my lunch but you can bring me a cup of ice for my soda, though."

"Okay, anyone else? Going once, going twice…" No one spoke up so she took Ms. Stella's list and made her way out the door to her car.

The sandwich shop was packed and the end of the line met her at the door. Standing in line was a task Cydney wouldn't take on so she jotted down the telephone number from the advertisement on the window and walked out calling their orders in. With time to waste she jumped in her car and shot across the street to the burger spot to get Yvette's cup of ice hoping it would be fully melted by her return.

"May I take your order?" a muffled male's voice asked through the static of the intercom.

"Yes, can I please have a large cup of ice?"

There was delay in response so she took the opportunity to retrieve her silver flask from the console between her seats and swallowed a mouthful of liquor. She wasn't an alcoholic but she needed a taste every now and then to mellow her out.

"Will that complete your order?"

"Yes, it will. Thank you," she said while taking deep breaths to chill the burn the liquor had placed on her throat.

"It's a $1.30 and you can pull up to the second window."

The sexiest man she had seen since she moved to Arizona met her at the pickup window. He was tall with dark skin and overflowing with handsomeness, but he was a fast-food worker, which she wouldn't even waste her time on by giving him further thought.

"That'll be a $1.30 beautiful," he said trying to conceal his smile not to reveal the gap he had between his front teeth.

"Here's two dollars and you can keep the change." Snatching the cup out of his hand, she drove off before he could get in full flirt mode. She pulled back in to the sandwich shop's parking lot and parked in the rear of the building facing a brick wall. Moving at the speed of lighting, she removed her suit coat and unfastened her pants. She allowed the liquor traced saliva to build a mass in her mouth until it tried to escape by slightly parting her full lips. With her mouth at full capacity, she placed her right index and middle finger in it and coated them with the watery warmth. There wasn't a need for her to pull her panties down because she never wore them. She rammed her fingers inside of her tunnel as she focused on the rock she was wearing on her free hand.

"I don't need a man for shit! Who can love me better than I already do?"

She said this chant every time she took the pleasure of pleasuring herself, which had been daily since her break up with Malik three summers earlier. She loved Malik but he drove through life at a turtle's pace and he was holding her back. There were too many opportunities she had to let fly by her because he wasn't ready for them.

If he would have lied to her or even gone as far as to cheat, she would have accepted it, but when it came to standing in the way of her hustle, she wouldn't have it. She had been raised by parents who thought a fried bologna sandwich with melted government cheese on it was a five-star meal. With her father becoming a full time crack consumer and her mother too lazy to get off her ass and get job, she vowed for more than what she saw in front of her. If it wasn't for her grandfather removing her from the hellhole she was raised in at 16 and instilling his hustling ways into her, she didn't know what would have become of her.

Grandpa Tim never touched nor sold a drug, yet his hustle game was off the charts. He screen printed t-shirts, set up bar-b-que stands at every public event he could, ran numbers, played the horses, cut hair, and that was just a small portion of his hustles. Grandpa Tim had only one goal set for Cydney and that was to strive to live life by the rules of Origami. He told her to get the paper, flip it, and fold it until she could make something beautiful out of it that she could call hers and that was exactly what Cydney had been doing. She knew if her grandfather were still alive, he would be proud of her for the position she held with the U.S. government. Now that he was gone, it saddened her to know that her guardian angel would never get his wings because all of her other hustles weren't as legal as her 8 to 5.

After living five long years without making progress in her origami lifestyle, she gave Malik his walking papers, a decision she'd always regret but wouldn't lose sleep over. If there was a way for her to fix things, she would, but time travel hasn't been invented yet. The only way she'd ever reunite with her one true love was by buying the grave plot next to his.

Malik had known too many of her secrets and she couldn't leave herself open to causalities from a man scorned, so she had his time on Earth terminated. Dealing with her mixed emotions of ordering the killing of the husband she never had threw her hustle off more, and once she got herself back on track she vowed to close her heart to love and only open her legs out of lust.

"No one can love me better than I do!" she said finally answering her own question.

She dug deeper inside of herself until she found the spot Malik had marked as his. She hit it with all the power she could muster while in a seated position until she felt her heart beat speed up. Her eyes began to flutter and she knew that her orgasm was just a few strokes away. As her phone rang to inform her that her order was ready, her fingers shot out of her at the eruption of her geyser.

"Yesss…" her shaky voice screamed out.

Her voicemail accepted the call on her behalf as she removed the lid on Yvette's cup of ice and cleaned the love juice off her fingers in it. *God, I hate that bitch,* she thought as a sinister smile graced her face..

Paper Planes

"Dafuq?" a customer frowned his face up at the drink machine. He took the lid off of his cup and peeked inside. "This ice water taste like pussy...Aye Michelle!" He turned towards the clerk who was behind the counter with her attention glued to the screen of her phone. She looked up at him and rolled her eyes. "God I hate that bitch," he said as he dumped out the contents of the cup.

D-Rock shook his head with a smirk as he walked past the man and stood at the counter. He just needed to grab a few things before his trip...his one-way flight to Phoenix. He hated how things had played out, but it was necessary for survival. Every street dude claims that they'd never snitch, until they are actually sitting on the wrong side of that desk. He was caught moving a key of coke to Virginia for Unc. As soon as he crossed into the town of Emporia, a place known for its overly strict traffic laws, he was pulled over for doing five miles above the limit. What should've been just a ticket, turned into the cop smelling weed in the car, giving them the probable cause to search the vehicle.

D-Rock nearly shitted on himself when he was told that he was facing a decade. Hearing dudes say they just did ten years was one thing, but seeing it on paper right in front of your face, was very different. They offered him a deal and he took it. He traded coworkers for his freedom. It was survival of the fittest, meaning not the strongest, but the fastest…the fastest one to take the deal is the one who survived.

He paid for his cigarettes and exited the store. As he walked across the parking lot, he took a minute to take in the scenery.

"Stop!" North Carolina was a beautiful place, but it wasn't home. AZ was home, and under the circumstances, D-Rock would gladly trade in the green pine trees- "Shut up, Bitch!" for the desolate deserts of Arizona. He hadn't been there in years, but he still had a lot of family in the area. "Josh, please don't do this. Please stop hitting me!" It wouldn't take long for D-Rock to get settled in with his new life, and he looked forward to the fresh start. "Bitch, I should kill your stupid ass right here!" So, it was farewell NC, and hello Ari- "Please stop!" D-Rock paused and looked over to the far corner of the lot. A scene was going and it had broken his train of thought.

"Shut the fuck up!" a small guy in a hood with his back towards D-Rock screamed. A woman was curled up on the ground, using her arms and legs to defend herself from his blows. D-Rock looked, but decided it wasn't his business. He was about to walk away until he heard a thunderous slap land on flesh, and the cries of a distressed female. He paused, stuffed his cigarettes in his back pocket, and turned back towards the situation. The guy was standing over the girl with his fist clenched up ready to strike again. "I should kill yo' ass!" They were positioned between a van with the side door open and another car on the other side. D-Rock knew that he should've just walked away, but seeing a woman being abused in public was something that he just couldn't ignore.

"Aye, bruh. Chill on all that. Especially out here, feel me?" D-Rock said as he stepped closer. The guy in the hoodie didn't even turn and face him. He just held his finger up over his shoulder.

"You might wanna mind your fucking business, before you become my business. You feel that?" the guy said, still towering over the girl. She looked up at him in fright, and then at D-Rock.

"Please, just go. He's crazy," she warned.

D-Rock couldn't let that slide. The guy was short and from the looks of it, not very muscular. He knew if it came down to it, he could surely beat the shit out of the guy. D-Rock sighed and walked over. His heartbeat was thumping chaotically so he took a deep breath and tried to settle himself. "Listen dude...you not about to be hitting no woman. Not in front me at least," D-Rock said as he stood behind the dude who still failed to turn and face him. "Since you wanna be a bully, let me show you what them blows feel like." He was waiting till the guy faced him and then he was going to ring his bell like Anita Ward.

Maybe he'd win the girl and score some pussy of appreciation before his farewell flight.

The guy pulled his hood off his head, turned towards D-Rock and said, "He's right here! Now which one of you is going to pay me and my girl?" There was a pause in the air as if the earth stopped. D-Rock looked in front of him and immediately recognized Wink getting out the car, as he winked at him with a smirk. Before D-Rock could take off running from the trap, a voice came from the inside of the van to his left. "Your heart was in the right place..." He turned and saw Brass step out. "But not your mind." The last thing D-Rock saw were the brass knuckles gleaming through the air, right before they made contact with his temple and flicked off his light switch.

*****

"Wake up, baby boy..." D-Rock opened his eyes gradually; graduating to the reality that he was about to be forced to drop out of existence. The throbbing in his head felt like California aftershocks. After a few blinks, his vision came into focus, and he immediately tried to stand up and flee for his life. His lack of strength was no match for the rope that wrapped around his chest and bound his arms behind him to the wooden chair. Just seeing Brass leaning in his face smiling with pupils of malevolence forced D-Rock to recollect on why he was truly there. He was so close...almost home, like a third base sprint, only to be called out for treason. All he had to do was mind his business and he would have been on a flight out of NC. His heart betrayed him, and now he was tied up in the middle of an abandoned warehouse, staring the Grim Reaper right in his eyes. "There he goes!" Brass said with excitement as he snapped his fingers in D-Rock's face.

D-Rock tried to speak but his mouth was gagged with some type of cloth and duct taped over it. Wink walked over into his frame of vision. He rocked the same stoic facial expression as he always did. D-Rock hated himself for falling for the trap. He closed his eyes and shook his head violently, as if he was trying to wake himself up from a lucid nightmare. Brass watched him and chuckled as he turned to Wink. "I think he is ready to talk. What you think?" Wink looked at D-Rock and then to Brass. He pulled a fixed blade knife from the pocket of his hoody and tapped the side of his jeans with it anxiously. "Let's see," Brass said as he snatched the duct tape from D-Rock's mouth, ripping hairs from his mustache and goatee with it. D-Rock spat the cloth from his mouth in disgust.

"Arrrrrrgggggghh!" D-Rock shouted from the pain. He looked around the vacant room and screamed to the top of his lungs. "Heeeeeeeeelp! Somebody he-" his plea was cut short when he felt his jaw shift and the legs of the chair rip from under him. One of the chair legs broke off and D-Rock tried to keep an eye on it. He landed on his back and Brass pounced on top of his chest with his fist cocked for another assault.

"Stop all that screaming, bitch!" Brass' humor was gone and he was in kill mode. "Your fucking mouth is what got you into this mess!" Brass swung again with the brass knuckles and blessed D-Rock with free dental work as he removed his wisdom tooth and the neighboring one as well. D-Rock nearly choked when the bone and blood tried to slide down his throat. His eyes watered, but another strike helped him with that as well as his face shifted to the left. He spat out the debris onto the dusty floor next to him, and braced himself for another punch. "I never trusted your bitch ass!" Brass was about to hit him again, but the front door swung open.

"An unconscious man can't speak," Unc said as he walked in wearing a navy-blue suit that fit his burly build perfectly. He stopped and adjusted his maroon tie. "And neither can a dead one..." Reece closed the door behind them after he took a final peek to make sure that nobody had followed them. Unc walked up with Reece as Brass climbed off of D-Rock and wiped the blood off his weapon onto his gray t-shirt.

"Isn't that the point?" Brass asked as he and Wink stood to the side. "To kill him so he can't talk?"

"Not before we find out what he's already told the police, dumbass," Reece commented. Brass glared at him but bit his tongue out of respect for the boss...plus he had a point.

"D-Rock...old friend, how goes it?" Unc asked. He signaled for Wink to bring him a chair from the other side of the room. Wink ran, retrieved the item, unfolded it, and stepped back into position. Unc sat down and rolled D-Rock over with an extension of his foot. "Cut him loose," Unc ordered Wink. Once D-Rock was free, he held his swollen face and sat on his ass. He looked pitiful, and for a second Reece felt bad for him, but his pain was deserved. He ordered his fate and tried to dine-and-dash. Now his past had caught up to him, and it was time to pay the bill.

"Unc...listen I-" the bottom of Unc's shoe colliding with his chin interrupted his statement.

"Don't you fucking call me Uncle. We are not family!" Unc spat. D-Rock tried to prop himself up on his elbow and hold his arm out to avoid getting kicked again. Brass came from the side and struck him in the chin, nearly disconnecting his jaw from his face.

"Put your fucking hands down when you speak to him!" Brass shouted. D-Rock lied face first on the floor, nearly paralyzed from agony. He decided to just stay there in that position. It was obvious he wasn't going to live through his current scenario. He accepted his fate.

"Ten years sure goes by quick when you are snitching, huh?" Unc asked. D-Rock remained silent and slowly closed his eyes. He was ready for it to be over with. Brass kicked him in the side, and it felt like a defibrillator on his chest as his eyes shot open.

"Now is not the time to shut your mouth, fuck boy! You should've been did that!" Brass said as he kicked him again.

"Chill, nigga. You're going to kill the bastard," Reece said softly as he pointed at D-Rock.

"Shut up, nigga. Let me handle this. This is the dirty side of the business that you don't specialize in," Brass countered.

"I'm just saying…"

"Don't say shit. They don't give degrees for this street shit. So stay in your lane, suit. Focus on your paperwork. This is my world, you are just visiting."

"Whatever, Brass…" Reece said as he crossed his arms and shook his head. He didn't have the energy to battle it out with Brass at the moment.

"Yeah, you damn right. It's whatever."

"Will you two shut the fuck up?" Unc snapped. He removed his tie and wiped the beads of sweat from his head with it. "Every time you are together you bicker like two little bitches."

"Listen…" D-Rock murmured. "I had to give them something. But I didn't rat on you, Unc…I swear."

"A rat is still a rat, no matter his diet." Unc folded his damp tie up and shoved it into his pocket. "But I'm curious. Who did you give up?" The room grew quiet as they waited for an answer. Unc already had his. The hesitation was all the truth he needed.

"A few Wilson niggas and the VA connect. That's it…I swear!" D-Rock said. Unc sighed and stood to his feet. Brass and Wink watched as he stepped over D-Rock and slowly made his way towards the door with Reece. Brass was a bit confused by the mute exit, so he called out to him.

"Aye, Unc! What do you want me to do with him?"

"Do your fucking job, nigga," Reece said as he turned and smiled at Brass. Unc spun around and looked over the place. He often used the building as a stash point, so he didn't want it contaminated with the blood of a rat.

"Just not in here," Unc said as he and Reece exited. Brass shook his head and turned to Wink. He wanted to be offended by always being tasked to do the dirty work of the operation, but he had to admit that he enjoyed it. Killing niggas felt better than sliding in new pussy that you worked 90 days to get. It was a rush. His balls tightened up with every jaw he broke, and every life he claimed.

"Let's get this nigga up," Brass nodded to Wink. They leaned over and lifted D-Rock up off of the floor. They marched him over to the door as he hunched over in pain. They planned on stuffing him in the trunk and taking him to one of their murder spots. As soon as they opened the door, D-Rock pulled the broken chair leg from under his shirt and stabbed Brass in the buff of his chest like he was Buffy the vampire slayer. The stake wasn't sharp enough to kill him, but the surprise attack knocked Brass to his ass. That was enough room for D-Rock to take off running towards the highway that he could hear on the other side of the buildings.

Wink looked at Brass for a second in shock. "Nigga! Fuck me; I'm a'ight. Go get that nigga!" Brass shouted as he tried to stand to his feet. Wink took off in full sprint behind his prey. D-Rock grimaced with each step, but he knew that he couldn't let his legs give out. He kept running, as blood leaked from his forehead and blinded one of his eyes. Still he pressed forward. He could hear Wink closing in on him so he pushed harder. He made it past the buildings and stepped onto the highway. The sun wasn't out, but the Gods smiled upon him. A squad car slammed on its breaks nearly inches from turning D-Rock into road kill.

Thinking maybe he was seeing things, D-Rock tried to continue running, but his legs folded beneath him. He fell to the asphalt and rolled to his back. His chest heaved for oxygen as he opened his eyes and saw the cop standing over him. He was safe…

"You ok?" the cop asked. His partner got out of the car and stopped traffic to protect his partner and the victim.

"They are going to kill me…" D-Rock mumbled.

"Who? Who is trying to kill you, son?" the older white cop asked. D-Rock lifted his arm and pointed in the direction that he came from. The cop looked, stood up and the squatted back down beside him. "There is nobody there. If there was, they are gone now. You're safe. Now let's get you to a hospital."

*****

Reece dropped Unc off at his door. Unc paused before he stepped out of the car and turned to Reece. "Nephew, come see me in the morning. Bring your ideas or whatever you have, and I'll listen." Reece smiled into the mirror at this glimmer of progression. "I can't promise I'll jump on anything, but I'll listen, ok?" Unc said as he squeezed Reece's shoulder. He nodded in appreciation. "Where in the hell is D?" Unc questioned as he noticed that her vehicle wasn't in its normal spot.

"Ladies night, remember?" Reece said as he glanced at his watch. Unc nodded and exited the car. Reece waited till he was safely in the house and pulled off. He now had his chance. He had been hounding Unc for years to hear him out on business ventures. Now he finally had his chance. The only problem was that he didn't really have any solid lanes to explore. He needed to come up with something quickly or lose his shot. Unc would never entertain the theory again if he showed up to the meeting with bullshit ideas.

Reece pulled into his driveway and exited his vehicle. As he walked down his driveway towards his subtle brick home, he slid his fingers over the red convertible BMW that was parked in front of his car. He smiled and opened the door. As he walked down his hallway, he removed his coat and pulled his shirttail from his jeans. He undid his belt and stepped into his bedroom with a smile stolen from the Grinch. Lying on the bed, in pink-laced lingerie was DeAndrea…

~

Unc sat in his office at his oversized oak desk. He had a glass of Remy Martin to his right with two ice cubes in it. He lifted the glass and took a small swig as the contents burned his throat on the way down. A cigar idled in the ashtray as trails of smoke slithered to the ceiling. He was relaxing, enjoying peace, and relieved that the problem with the rat was on its way to being settled. Unc knew that he was getting long in the tooth. His body couldn't handle the street life anymore. The things that he once enjoyed, he now dreaded. He was tired of the bloodshed, and at age 55, all he wanted to do was spend his golden years on the sands of a private beach somewhere. Maybe Reece had the right idea with going legit…Unc raised the cigar to his lips. "That kid has his head in the right place."

~

Reece had his head right in place, between DeAndrea's thighs. His hands massaged her breasts as he whispered secrets through her clit. She leaned back on her elbows in ecstasy as he tortured her

42

soul with bliss. Their relationship had started a while ago, and at first, it was just a mistake. Reece was playing driver again and dropped D off at home when she got too drunk at a party once. Once inside, she pulled him on top of her as she collapsed on the couch and went for his dick. He wanted to stop her out of respect for his boss and her drunken state, but he didn't. Truth was he'd wanted her ever since he first laid eyes on her. He fucked her as if he loved her on her husband's couch, and within those cushions, their relationship became firm.

Reece slid his tongue up her torso and to her breast. He circled around the soft flesh and landed on her nipple. She moaned from the warm sensation of his mouth. He loved pleasing her by any means, even though what they shared wasn't love at all; it was pure lust. As he nibbled on her nipples, she became crippled when he slid his dick inside of her expectantly. Unc never made love to her like that. He fucked her. He would bend her over and stroke her for about five minutes, and then roll over into a slumber. Reece took his time. He explored her body with his tongue and her abandoned tunnel with his dick. He stroked her slowly, passionately, circularly, turning her hole into an oval with his width.

He stared into her eyes as she came, and kissed her while gently biting on her bottom lip. Her legs started to tremble as she climaxed. This triggered Reece to pull her legs up on his shoulders, fully opening up her pussy as he dug deep in her channel. She screamed and rocked her head side to side, as another orgasm followed the first like tremors. "Reece!" He loved it when she called his name. He sped his strokes up, swimming in her wetness, and drowning in her moans. She grabbed the pillow to mute herself, but he snatched it from her teeth and slung it across the room.

"Tell the world who this pussy belongs to!" he said as he wrapped his arms under her shoulders and went rabbit mode in her rabbit hole, taking them both into another dimension. Her eyes rolled back as he pulled out and ejaculated all over her stomach. He sat there on his knees, panting with his hands on his hips as his dick throbbed and slowly softened into its natural form. DeAndrea smiled, grabbed a cloth from the nightstand, and cleaned herself up.

"You should've came inside me," she said. Reece raised a brow.

~

Unc raised a brow. He thought he heard something so he stood up and peeked out of the window. The glass dropped from his grasp and shattered against the wooden floor. Scattered across his lawn were police vehicles and a SWAT team van. Before he could even react, the door to his office was kicked off the hinges and three cops tackled him to the floor.

He couldn't believe what was going on. He had been extremely careful throughout his entire career. What did they have on him? D-Rock was dead, so they had nothing. Probably just angered 'because they lost their witness. Unc smiled and relaxed as they stood him to his feet in handcuffs. "Call my lawyer, muhterfuckers! You don't have shit on me!"

A detective walked over to him and smiled as he unfolded a sheet of paper and scanned over it. "We got you for the attempted murder of Dante Rock...aka D-Rock. How's that sound?" the detective asked. Unc frowned his face up and whispered to himself.

"Attempted?"

"Yup...your hitmen let him get away and now the shit storm that we were waiting to bring to your doorstep has been upgraded." The detective smiled and folded the paper up into an airplane. "Now I have enough to put you away till your twilight years," the detective said as he tossed the paper plane across the office. It soared and landed right on the desk in front of a wedding photo of Unc and DeAndrea.

~

DeAndre's phone was blowing up, but she ignored it as always. She was in her comfort zone, and didn't want to leave. She was wrapped up in the arms of her man, well not her man, but the man who should be her man...at least that's how she felt. "When are we going to stop hiding?" she asked softly. Reece opened his eyes and looked at her.

"What do you expect me to do? Come forward and get killed for messing with Mr. Biggs' girl?" he joked and tried to kiss her but she turned away. She wasn't in a joking mood.

"I'm serious, Reece. I want us to be together, and if you want the same then you need to make it happen. I don't wanna keep living this charade. I don't like being the side chick."

"Actually...I'm the side chick," Reece said as he broke out into a chuckle. DeAndrea stood up and started getting dressed with fury painted on her face. That was the one thing that she hated about Reece; he could be immature at times. "Where are you going?" Reece asked as he sat up. He noticed that now his phone was blowing up. It was too late for it to be a casual call, so he knew that it had to be important. Still he couldn't answer it till he made things right with DeAndrea. "Come here, baby," he said as he stood up and wrapped her in his arms. "I wish things were different, but you and I both know that there is no way out of this. I'm a man of ideas, but what can we possibly do?"

DeAndrea looked up into his eyes and said, "Kill him."

Reece let her go and walked to the other side of the room to retrieve his phone. "I'ma act like I didn't hear that. You must be high or some shit, D."

"You must be scared or some shit, Reece," she said as she pinned her hand on her hip.

"Listen, fucking you is bad enough. I'm not going to kill my boss, my mentor, my *friend*, just so we can be together. That's not love, that's craziness, D!" he shouted as he dialed the number back that had called him. He shook his head at her as she stood at the doorway.

"Maybe we just have two different ideas of love then," she said as she exited.

Reece shook his head and focused on the strange number that had been blowing him up. "Hello?"

"Mr. Reece? This is David Macomb," the voice said.

"Yeah, the lawyer, what's up?" Reece asked as he stood to his feet, expecting the worst.

"They got him…"

No FAQ

"Damn, what took you so long?"

Yvette was sitting in Cydney's chair with her eyes focused on the slide show that served as her screensaver.

"Who is this ugly ass rabbit teeth nigga you're all hugged up with? I assumed you had better taste in men," Yvette said with a laugh.

Cydney closed the door behind her and locked it.

"Look bitch, let's stop this fake ass being cordial shit, it's gone on long enough. You don't like me and I can't stand you. What in the fuck are you doing in my office?"

"What's already known doesn't need to be said, ho!" Yvette said while placing her bare feet on the desk and crossing her legs before she continued. "And this was my office first or did you forget?"

Cydney track starred her way across the room; snatched Yvette up by her overly baby oiled legs, and yanked her out of her chair. She hit the floor with a thud.

"No ho, you must've forgotten that I took your spot!" Cydney said as Yvette got to her feet.

They stood toe to toe in each other's faces silently like two boxers at the weigh-in, both breathing heavily. Cydney set her food and the cup of ice down just in case Yvette wanted to upgrade the verbal confrontation to a physical one.

"Yeah you took it," Yvette said grabbing the cup of ice and removing the lid off of it. After inspecting it for miscellaneous extras, she shook a small amount of it into her mouth and chewed. "But please know I'm on a mission to get it back. You may have the office fooled into thinking your holier than thou but bitch I'm not moved!" She took the long way around the desk so she wouldn't have to pass Cydney.

"Well, let me help you get moved." She picked up the cheap black heels Yvette left under her desk and torpedoed them at her. "Don't come for me unless I call on you, bitch, and even then, you may want to forward me to voicemail. Enjoy your ice!"

Yvette spit the remaining ice out of her mouth and threw the cup at her as if it burned a hole into her hand. She ran out of the office to the safety of their co-workers just in case she needed witnesses to Cydney's madness.

Cydney stopped herself from running out of the office after her because she knew that was exactly what she wanted her to do. If she showed her ass in front of their co-workers, Yvette would win and she wasn't built to take losses. She began cleaning up the ice that covered her desk with malice in her heart as her door re-opened.

"Senorita Adore, I was told you wanted to see me." A young short muscular man of Latin decent entered her office with fear written all over his face.

"Oh yes, Jorge, I do need to see you but you know better than to meet me here. Meet me at seven at our usual place; now get the fuck out of my face!"

Jorge closed her door and stepped farther into her office.

"No disrespect Senorita but I feel safer with meeting you here, especially after what you've done to me and my wife."

"I didn't do anything to you or your wife Jorge," she chuckled. "Anything that has happened to you and your family falls on your shoulders. We had a deal and you broke it. You're not to be trusted and I refuse to discuss this with you here. I'll see you at seven, adios!"

Once again, ignoring her request for him to leave, he brushed the ice off the chair in front of her desk and then sat down.

"But here is where you can fix my problem," he said with his head down to avoid the daggers her eyes had become. "Please Senorita, I can't live here without my wife, and she is pregnant."

"Boo-fucking-who. You should have thought about that before you decided to ignore my calls. I had her deported because you were hiding from me. Didn't I tell you I'm God when it comes to you living in America? You took my words lightly so I had no choice but to show you. As a matter fact," she said pulling a file out of her top drawer. "I was just in the process of denying you citizenship and shipping your ass back for the stunt you pulled. Did you really think I wouldn't find out?"

Confusion crossed his face, "Find out what? I give you thirty percent of everything I earn like we agreed."

"Liar!" she yelled as a trickle of spit flew out of her mouth like fire from a dragon. "Our agreement was that I grant you citizenship as long as I get thirty percent of every dollar you make in America while you go through citizenship classes. But you failed to keep that agreement."

Jorge dug in his pocket and produced every check stub from every temp assignment he had been sent on. "Here's proof!" he said handing them to Cydney but she wouldn't accept them.

"The money that you made on the side didn't come with a check stub, Jorge!"

Shock replaced the look on his face. He wondered how she could have known about the drugs he was trafficking for his cousin. He didn't tell a soul about the trips he took, not even his wife.

"God knows all!" she said as if she read his mind. "You moved cocaine from Mexico to the United States and received pay for doing so on U.S. soil. Where's my money?"

"Senorita, I did not know..."

She cut him off. "Keep lying and I'll cut your tongue out your fucking mouth and wipe my ass with it! You have two options for deportation at this point. You can give me my 30-fucking-percent and I'll put you on a bus back home or you can tell me you don't have it and I'll ship your corpse back to Mexico inside a donkey shaped piñata via the Rio Grande. The choice is yours."

Jorge remained silent. He had her thirty percent but paying her wouldn't keep him from being deported. It would only keep him alive.

"You don't have all day to decide!" she shouted.

Standing up at her words, he lifted his shirt and revealed the money. It was wrapped and taped around his lower abdomen like a WWE championship title belt.

"This is everything I made from the trips, forty thousand dollars. Your fee and my earnings are all here. I will give it all to you if you don't deport me and allow my wife to return, please senorita."

Like a kid driving past McDonalds, Cydney's eyes lit up at the beautiful paper in front of her. He could've had a hundred dollars in ones wrapped around him and she would have had the same reaction to it. Like her grandfather always said, "Pennies can turn into nickels, nickels become dimes, dimes to quarters and if you're folding that paper right baby, you'll sho'nuff see some dollars." Knowing that to be true, she wiped up the small puddle of water the ice made on her desk with Jorge's denial paperwork.

"I'll take the money from you this time and get your wife back on the next thing heading our way, but there's something I need you to do for me. Go get Tomas and tell him his time in the United States is up!"

******

Tomas knew his work visa would expire soon but he assumed that all of the extra work he had been doing for Senorita Adore would ensure its renewal. He had become her right-hand man, her move maker, and her sexual play toy whenever she felt childishly erotic.

He had moved to the United States from El Salvador to help his little brother Julio's blue collar staffing agency flourish. The agency gave general laborers daily assignments and pay but Julio had more contract workers than he had business contracts. With Tomas as his business partner, he knew that would change.

Julio had obtained citizenship when he married his American wife while in college. Now that he was a degree holder and the money was in place he was ready to fully live the American dream, but he needed his brother's help. Tomas didn't attend college, he took his classes in the pave-less streets of El Salvador, but he was the most successful businessman Julio had known. He thought he could take his older brother's street smarts and combine them with the education he received at N.Y.U. to become a powerhouse in New York. The only problem Julio had foreseen was getting his brother to the U.S. legally and that's when they met Senorita Adore.

There wasn't anything spectacular about the immigration officer when Julio met her at the field office but Tomas' eyes had seen more. Cydney's dark brown skin color looked smooth to the touch and was in need of being touched. He could tell by the emptiness in her bubbly eyes, which were identical in color to her skin that she lacked every form of love there is. In his mind, her full lips were calling out to him, welcoming his kisses, and wanting him to rescue her from the world.

She was bigger than most of the girls he had been attracted to back home yet none of them held a candle to her curvaceous shape. The entire time that Cydney spent explaining the terms of his work visa to him, he battled the urge to run his finger through her shoulder length hair. He wanted to ball her hair up in the palm of his hand, yank her back with so much force that if he wasn't careful he'd break her neck, and sloppily tongue kiss her until their mouths tasted the same.

This was a first for Tomas, he had never had his attention peaked by a black woman before. He wasn't a cup of caramel himself but even with his dark roasted peanut skin color, he knew his brown pride was not the same as hers. It wasn't until he remembered that he didn't speak English did his thoughts of getting close to Cydney fade away.

"Do you understand and accept these conditions?" she asked finally looking up at the sexy brown-skinned warrior in front of her.

"I'm sorry ma'am but my brother doesn't speak any English but I can act as an interpreter if you want," Julio chimed in.

She exhaled deeply and turned back to the first page.

"No, I got it," she said and started reading the document to him again but this time in Spanish. Tomas couldn't contain his excitement and nudged his brother in disbelief.

"Como aprendiste espanol?" he asked in his native tongue cutting her off in midsentence but she continued to read as if he hadn't said a word. When she was done and he accepted and signed the terms she said, "I speak several languages and I taught myself all of them. Welcome to America, Tomas."

Tomas floated out of her office vowing to do whatever was necessary to make Senorita Adore his. He never imagined that would mean committing constant acts that could jeopardize his freedom and his life. However, he still did everything she had asked of him without hesitation. When she asked him to use her clients from the immigration office to fill open positions at his staffing agency, he did. When she asked him to open a new location in Arizona to help expand her hustle, he packed up and moved. And whenever she requested to feel the stubble from the regrowth around his mouth on her second pair of lips, he made sure to rub his face all in it. There wasn't anything he wouldn't do for Cydney and she knew it and often abused it.

It wasn't until he confessed his love to her and had it rejected, that Tomas realized they weren't more than business partners. So he moved on, which was a decision he thought had caused his work visa not to be renewed.

"Excuse me, but you can help me please?" Tomas asked the information clerk.

It was three minutes until closing and Yvette was in no mood to deal with another broken English-speaking client. She would have to call an interpreter to assist her and there was no way she was staying past five. She needed to shower and change so she could be at the airport to meet her cousin by seven.

"No sir, you come back tomorrow and I'll help you. I'm closed," she whispered praying Cydney hadn't heard her as she passed her window to exit the building.

"No, you help now...please. Tomorrow I get d... de...deee..." he began to stutter.

I know this motherfucka don't think I'm about to put up with his stuttering too, she thought as he continued.

"...deported."

"Shit, if you're going on the deportation list tomorrow you're already too late!" Yvette pulled down the metal window closure in Tomas's face and locked it. He banged on it pleading for Yvette's help but she picked up the phone instead.

"Security, can you please let the gentleman know it's five o'clock and we are now closed.

Thanks!" Laughing, she grabbed her purse and made her way to her car using the rear exit. She had planned on getting off before Cydney so she could key her car, that's why she always parked where there were no cameras, but she was long gone.

"Please Yvette, I need your help. That bitch is trying to deport me," a voice said behind her as she turned her key in the door.

To her surprise, it was the same guy she had refused to help. His English was perfect unlike before, but what puzzled her the most, was how he had known her name.

"Did Security give you my name?"

"No, Cydney did. That's the bitch who's trying to have me deported. I mentioned you were cute in my appointment with her and she went crazy on me."

Yvette smiled at the compliment he had given her.

"I'm sorry about that but she's very jealous of me. Come back when we open in the morning and I'll see what I can do for you."

She hurriedly got into her car, locked the doors, and cranked it up before he could respond. She never once gave thought to what happened to his accent or his stutter as she made it to the interstate.

She was two city blocks away from her house waiting for the light to turn green when her phone rang. She didn't recognize the number but she knew it was her cousin.

"Hey D-Rock, are you about to board your flight?" she asked with excitement in her voice. She hadn't seen her cousin since they were teenagers and she couldn't wait to rip through Phoenix with him. She could tell something was wrong with him but she decided not to question him about it until they were face to face. The only information he gave her by phone was that he had been jumped and it caused him to miss his previous flight. Him arriving in Arizona safely was her only concern.

"Wrong person, bitch!"

Yvette recognized Cydney's voice instantly.

"Bitch, why you tell that dude my name and what car I drive? You're a jealous, hatin' ass ho…"

When she realized her voice was echoing in her ear it was already too late. Cydney reached over the seat, grabbed Yvette by her wig, and almost severed her head from the body. Yvette's head fell back like the hood on a hoodie. Only the thick jugular veins on both sides of her neck kept her head attached. Reaching past the bleeding corpse in the driver's seat, Cydney put the car in park and hit the emergency lights then exited out the rear door. Tomas pulled up next to her like clockwork in her Benz and they drove off as the light turned green.

As she dropped the knife in the sack he had waiting for her and removed her gloves, she looked at Tomas shaking her head. "I still hate that bitch!"

He laughed reminiscing on the time when he couldn't speak a word in English and then said, "I'm just happy I'm not really getting d... de... dee...deported."

She joined in laughing at her own plan. *But hell, it worked*, she thought.

Paper Trails

"Get in here and shut the door," Unc said sternly as he stood behind his desk. Sitting in the plush leather seats across from him were Reece and Brass. Wink closed the heavy door gently and stood next to Brass with his hands folded in front of him. Unc had paid 10% of a fortune to make bail, but he knew that his time as a free man was coming to end. They had enough evidence on him to hit him with the triple digits if everything fell into place. If Unc had children, they would have to go to prison as well when they turned 18 to cover their father's debt.

D-Rock had given the authorities everything from drugs to murders. Unc tried his best to keep his hands free of blood in his organization, but that wasn't always the case. Some situations couldn't be handled like gentlemen, and demanded violence- this was one of those situations. "Boy, you really fucked this one up, didn't cha?" he asked rhetorically as he stared a hole into Brass' face. Wink lowered his head. "All you had to do was kill the little fuck!"

"Unc, on my good word, we had that nigga but-" Brass started.

"Mutherfucker! I know that! I was..." Unc lowered his voice and looked around the home office as if he feared that it was wired. He leaned his hefty body further over the desk towards Brass. "I was there. How you fucked that up is beyond me."

"The nigga stabbed me with a fucking dagger or some shit!" Brass said as he lifted his shirt to show his wound. Reece glanced over at the bandaged area that still had speckles of blood on it.

"I don't give a fuck!" Unc slammed his fist on the desk, making Reece flinch and devote his attention back to the boss man. "I pay you two niggas to keep shit like this from happening." Wink glanced up and quickly lowered his head again. Unc sighed and stood straight up as he turned and faced his bookshelf. "Now what are we going to do?" The room grew quiet. He snapped back around and stared at Reece. "Tell me!" he ordered as he flopped down in the enormous desk chair that resembled a throne in statue. His stare was never interrupted by a blink and finally Reece realized that he was really asking him a question.

"Ummmm, you asking me?" Reece inquired with a puzzled expression.

"Yes, you mutherfucker. You are the," Unc snapped his fingers, "advisor, right? You always want to throw in your two fucking cents. Well nigga here's the time to flip that fucking coin in the wishing well. Let's hear it."

Reece hesitated as he gathered his thoughts. Brass would love it if the blame could somehow be shifted. He waited silently for his nemesis to fumble with his words and crack under pressure. "Well, I think it's simple. Find D-Rock and neutralize the threat. We do that and all of this goes away."

"That simple, huh?" Brass interjected, knowing that he'd end up doing the dirty work. Not that he minded, but he didn't like taking orders from Reece.

"Yeah, just this time you two knuckleheads have to actually man up and do your job."

Brass stood to his feet with his fist clenched. "I'll show you a fucking knuckle, my nigga!" Reece shot up to his feet and stood in Brass' face, fearless, and ignorant to how crazy Brass actually was.

"Y'all sit the fuck down!" Unc commanded. The two men stalled, neither one wanting to be the first to back down. "Now!" Unc shouted. He didn't have time for Cain and Abel to quarrel. "All of our freedom is on the line, and you two want to have a pissing contest." Reece sat down and Brass followed suit with a cold stare.

"Like I was saying," Reece started.

"It's not that easy. I got word that the little slick fuck is under protection till he flies out to Phoenix. The next time I'll see him is in the courtroom, and the rabbit will have the gun then." Unc looked off into space and shook his head in disappointment. "How in the hell did it come to this? They don't make niggas out of the same fabric as they used to."

"We can go get him…" Reece offered. Brass shot him a look.

"What do you mean? Go get him? In Phoenix?" Unc asked. Reece nodded with a grin.

"Nigga, you know how big Phoenix is?" Brass threw in. He knew that 'we' meant him and Wink. "How in thee fuck do you expect Wink and I to find one man in a city of like…" he looked up to gather a guesstimate. "A city of like a billion people…"

"Nigga, let me handle the thinking part of this. I'm better at it. Now if you'd listen more than you ran you fucking trap, you'd pick up on information like I do. I have the nigga's mother's address," Reece announced. Unc raised a brow. Brass snapped his head towards him. Wink looked up. The grand clock on the wall continued to tick…time was running out.

"What makes you think he will go to his mother's house? Out of all the places to go. Knowing we are looking for him. Huh?" Brass pointed at Unc. "Right, Unc?"

"He has a point, Reece," Unc said. "Why would he go there? It's a big city. I dunno about a billion folks, but it's a big city."

"A billion if you count the Mexicans," Brass said. Wink broke character and snickered, but a look from Unc killed the humor.

"If you just traded in your manhood and pride to save your own miserable ass, who would you run to for them to kiss your wounds?" Reece held his palms out waiting for an answer. "D-Rock was an only child. Like me...trust me, he'll go to Mama." Brass shook his head. Wink lowered his. Unc nodded his head, and the clock kept ticking.

"You're right," Unc said as he leaned back in the chair. He looked at Brass and Wink. "Make it happen. Quickly!" he said as he pointed. "And make sure he's fucking dead this time. All of our asses are on the line."

"So what? We just hop a flight. Go there, and blend in like tourists, or some shit?" Brass questioned.

"No flights. Tickets make a paper trail...paper trails fold into cases," Reece said.

"Drive?" Brass' eyes widened in shock. "Nigga it would take like 4 days! That's if we don't get lost. The damn trial might fucking start by the time we get there!" Brass said as he shook his head.

"It will take 32 ½ hours," Reece said. Unc glanced at him pleasantly. Reece had entertained this idea the night before, so he had a few facts. "That includes avoiding tolls or any other kind of paper trail."

"Make it happen," Unc said in closing. Brass looked at Reece, stood to his feet, and exited with Wink as he shook his head. As Reece was about to leave and start his job on locating a low-key rental service, Unc grabbed his arm.

"Reece, be careful out there, you hear me?" Reece nodded. "I see you as a son, and I don't have to express how I'd feel if something happened to you, do I? Good. But understand that this is important. D-Rock must fall, or we will." Reece nodded and walked towards the door. "I haven't forgotten, Reece." Reece paused with his hand on the knob. "When this is over, we are going to sit down and go over your business ideas. How do you say it? Making something out of this paper?" Reece turned towards him and smiled as he exited the room and closed the door behind him.

Once he made it down the steps, DeAndrea grabbed his arm and pulled him into the kitchen. Reece looked around to make sure that Brass and Wink were gone, and that Unc was still in his office. "Why are you doing this?" she whispered. Reece frowned his face up. "Helping him. Why are you doing it? Don't you see that this is our chance to get rid of him?"

"This isn't the way, D. Not like this." He turned to leave but she sidestepped in front of him.

"Why not? Sounds perfect to me. He goes to prison, you take over the business, and…"

"D!" Reece said through gritted teeth as he grabbed her shoulders. "You sound real trife right now. Listen to yourself."

"Oh, I'm trifling?" she asked as she leaned her head back in shock.

"This isn't how we do it…"

"Why not? Cause you got some other bitch on your mind? Huh? You don't wanna be with me, do you? This was all just some game to you, I see…" Her voice was rising so Reece peeked around the corner cautiously.

"If he goes to prison, we all go with him. You included. There will be no business left to run…there will be no us. You understand?" She looked into his eyes and found sincerity.

"Ok, whatever…" she sassed as she turned away. Reece watched for a few seconds.

"We'll talk later. I don't have time right now, ok?" Reece offered. She still had her back to him.

"Time is like money, it's expendable…but it all depends on what you make out of it," she said as she left the kitchen and disappeared down the hall.

*****

"Man, y'all fuckers quiet as shit. I'ma fuck around and fall sleep," Brass said as he steered the rental down the highway. Wink was in the back, staring out the window at the scenery, just taking it all in. It was an experience for him. Before that moment, he had never left the state of North Carolina. He was on a blood trip to mend his wrongs, and the wrongs of others, but the ride was nice. He sank deeper into the seat and continued his admiration.

Reece rode in the passenger seat, keeping a watchful eye on Brass and his antics. He monitored his laptop, and their routes, carefully avoiding tolls, traffic stops, accidents, and other hiccups in their journey. They were less than an hour out, and he was ready to get it over with and have the problem that was set to blow up in their face defused. If everything went according to plan, or at least close to it, Reece would gain a lot of respect and trust from Unc. Hopefully now he'd listen to him and take the leap of faith, the calculated step out of the drug game and on to something legit. Reece tapped the tip of a pen against his chin. *But what, though?*

Brass plugged his phone into the AUX port and went to scrolling through his music app. Reece looked over at him when he felt the car shift a bit. "Hold on, I got some shit for y'all niggas. Some theme music, you feel me?" Brass said with a grin as he took his remaining hand off the wheel and rubbed it through his short fro. He pressed play and placed the phone on his knee as he cranked the volume up. The speakers in the Chevy Impala blared and rattled Reece's eardrums.

"Running through the six with my woes…" Brass sung a long with Drake's *Know Yourself*, as if the rumors Quentin Miller ghostwrote the lyrics for him didn't exist. He beat the steering wheel like the song had pulled him into a trans with its truths. Reece had to look at him to see if he had in fact gone crazy. "Counting money, you know how it goes!" his eyes closed as his head rocked side to side.

"Man, pay attention to the road with yo' shower singing ass," Reece said. Brass ignored the request and sung even louder.

"Pray the real live forever man!" he shouted in Reece's ear. "Pray the fakes get exposed," he recited as he poked Reece in the chest, sending a message with the lyrics.

"Nigga, stop playing. That's your fucking problem." Reece was beginning to get agitated now. It seemed like whenever Brass discovered a route to get under his skin, like a novice nurse finding a vein for an IV, he'd capitalize on it.

"I want that Ferrari, then I swerve!" Brass yanked the wheel and switched lanes like he was playing Frogger. Reece looked back at the vehicle that they swerved around to make sure it wasn't an unmarked police car. "I want that Bugatti just to hurt 'em!" Brass stomped on the gas as the engine roared. He was hitting speeds well over 90mph down the desert road. "I ain't rock my jewelry, that's on purpose," he said as he plucked the threads of his tank top.

"Brass! Chill the fuck out nigga! This ain't the time for you to be stupid!" Reece shouted over the music. He reached and tried to turn the volume down. Brass smacked his hand and pointed at him.

"Niggas want my spot and don't deserve it…" He held his stare, ignoring the road, as the car slowly drifted off the pavement. The sound of gravel hitting the bottom of the car broke his stunt as he snatched the wheel back and started laughing. "Chill out, nigga. You always so fucking serious and shit."

"That's what I'm supposed to be. Your problem is that you are never serious. You think everything is a fucking game, and it isn't. Now focus on the task at hand."

"Focus on the task at hand," Brass repeated. "This nigga always trying to sound all…all…all whatever the fuck you try to sound like. You not high and mighty, nigga." Wink shook his head in the backseat. He was getting tired of the two battling for power. They argued the entire ride, and it was ruining the tranquility of the experience for him. "Don't forget, you are the reason we are driving, ol' super cautious ass. We could've been there, killed the nigga, and on a flight back home already."

"Man, how stupid are you?" Reece asked. Brass scowled at him. "If that nigga turn up dead, who do you think will be the prime suspects? Don't hurt yourself thinking about it 'cause I'll tell you. Us! That's who. First thing they gon' do is check the flights to Phoenix. Match the timeframes up and bam!" Reece preached. He could tell that his words weren't getting through Brass' thick head. "This is bigger than Unc. Soon as they bring him up, they coming for you and Wink, and then myself. Remember, we all were there. We all played a part in what yo' ass fucked up."

Brass just shook his head. He was about to talk some more shit, but the upcoming sight froze him. With the mountains in the backdrop, the tall buildings and city lights looked like a scene from a movie. Even Wink leaned forward to get a better view of the city. "Damn..." Brass whispered. It was as if they had discovered a new continent. Phoenix made Rock City look like a trailer park just from the skyline alone.

"Who the fuck would leave this to come to Rock City?" Brass asked. Reece checked his laptop and got into 'Go' mode. The ride wasn't as bad as he thought, but it wasn't the time to celebrate or go sightseeing. As beautiful as the city was, they only had two agendas: Kill D-Rock, and get the fuck out of the city unseen.

"Doesn't matter why he left. We know why he returned." Reece looked at Brass and grinned. "A snitch with a paper trail…"

~

"Game time boys! Wink, do what you do." Brass said. Wink already knew what was up. He'd enjoyed the peace of the commute, but now it was time to earn his stripes and save his rep. He folded the backseat down and reached into the trunk. It took him a minute as he shuffled around through the bags, but finally he pulled out a black duffle bag and unzipped it. Inside it was an assortment of weapons, from pistols, to submachine guns, even a sniper rifle, which Wink had been dying to use. His facial twitch wouldn't stop shit once he got behind that scope. Brass watched through the mirror and smiled at his soldier, while Reece directed him through the city and towards their destination.

"We should hit a strip club while we are here, ya know?" Brass said as they cruised slowly through the congested traffic. Reece looked at him in disgust, as if he hadn't heard anything Reece had preached the entire ride. "Nigga, calm down. It was a joke," Brass said as he shook his head. He was becoming anxious and agitated in the city life Stop and Go traffic. Back in Rock City, it was never like that, but he had to remember that he was abroad. As much as he hated to admit it, Reece was right and they needed to stay low during their visit.

After about 30 minutes of driving through the city, they finally pulled into a neighborhood. The outer city was beautiful, but no matter where you were in America, every hood looked the same. There was always the same vibe, the same smell in the air that let you know that you just entered hell's territory. The only difference between this hood and the ones back in NC, was the fact that there were a lot of Mexicans...a lot. "You sure we in the right spot?" Brass asked as he kept his head on a swivel. "This don't feel right to me," Brass said as he reached his arm back towards Wink. Wink handed him a Glock 40 as Brass carefully placed it on his lap.

"This is the spot. Pull over right here," Reece said as he closed the laptop and stuffed it in his carrying case. Brass parked the car and kept a paranoid eye on everyone that he saw outside moving. In NC, if you're lucky, you might see one or two Hispanics out and about, but never on the level that Brass was witnessing at the moment. He felt like he had crossed the border by mistake. Next thing he knew, he'd be on some Cartel video with his head getting chopped off. "Two houses up. The green raggedy piece shit right there. You see it?" Reece asked. Brass nodded as Wink leaned forward for a glimpse. "Now we wait…"

The wait wasn't long but it felt like an eternity. Brass was exhausted but he'd come too far to get caught sleeping on the job again. They watched the house like thirsty detectives until finally, their nearly 33-hour investment paid off. Reece sprung forward and pointed as he repeatedly slapped Brass on the chest. "Look! Look!" he said elatedly like a child seeing snow for the first time. On the porch of the house that they had been staring at for so long they could draw it from memory, out stepped a familiar face…bruised face, but familiar. "Told you, niggas!" Reece said as he punched his palm. He couldn't hold back his smile because he honestly wasn't sure how credible his source of information really was. He took the intel on a hunch, and it paid off. Had it not, Brass and Wink would've probably 'accidently' killed him.

"A'ight, let's go handle this nigga!" Brass ordered as he cocked the pistol and reached for the door. Wink kicked open his door and was about to lunge out until Reece called out to them.

"Wait! We can't be stupid about this. Just chill a second…"

Brass slid back inside and gave Reece a dumbfounded look. "Listen, my nigga. Your job was to get us here, and I'll admit it, you did that shit. But don't get it twisted. When it comes to laying bodies down, I run that side of the business, you feel me?"

"Nah, my job is to make sure this gets done right, and flawlessly. Especially after you fucked up the last one." Reece met Brass' stare and didn't back down in posture. Brass was a knucklehead, but he knew the seriousness of the matter at hand. "Plus, you gon' shoot a man in front of his Mom Dukes?" Reece pointed as D-Rock embraced a lady in a tight hug. The Carolina visitors watched as D-Rock then hopped inside a Ford F-150, followed by a sketchy character that emitted a bad vibe all the way down the street and into Reece's heart. Reece didn't want to be responsible for claiming any other lives during their trip, but he was willing to do whatever it took to get the deed done and over with.

*****

D-Rock exited the taxi and glanced around the old hood. It felt good to be back, but under the circumstances, he couldn't stop looking over his shoulder. Unc was or should be in custody with his minions soon to follow. All D-Rock had to do was show up in court, testify, and he'd be a free man.

Free to start a new chapter in life and reinvent himself.

He slung his bags over his shoulders and approached the home, the same home that he was born in, raised in, and created so many memories in. Back then, he was an only child, growing up in a quiet house within a loud hood. When his aunt died, everything changed, his two cousins, Yvette and Jean-Paul were forced to move in with his mom and him. He and Yvette became close, as any cousins under the same roof would, but there was always a childish rivalry between him and JP, as any cousins under the same roof would have.

The main question now was, where in the hell was Yvette? She was supposed to be at the airport to pick him up, but of course, she wasn't. She had terrible time management skills, so he waited and called her phone for hours, still nothing. Finally, he just took a cab, and decided to surprise his mother that way. He vowed to choke Yvette till her head popped off when he saw her, especially if her forgetful ass was inside.

He grabbed the knob and gave it a slight twist. The doors were always unlocked because there was always someone home. He could hear the voices coming from the living room, so he eased the door shut behind him, dropped his bags, and stuck his head in. His mother was the first to see him. She had to lean forward a bit to make sure that her eyes weren't deceiving her, and finally she hopped up to her feet, ran over, and clutched her baby in a tight hug.

"Hey, Mama. How are you, lady?" he said with a smile as he wrapped his arms around her. JP was sitting on the couch with a weird look on his face. He sported a high-top fade, and a small gold chain that nearly choked him. He was always a scrawny character, but he seemed to have put on a few pounds since D-Rock had last seen him. Still hugging his mother, D-Rock nodded his head over at JP, but his cousin didn't return the notion. He just looked off into space as if something was really bothering him.

"I'm glad you are here, baby. I swear you couldn't have come at a better time," Mama Rock said as she let go of his chest and guided him into the living room by his hand. D-Rock could tell something bad had happened. The vibe in the room was stale. "Have you heard what happened to Yvette yet, baby?" Mama Rock asked as she sat down and cleared a spot on the couch next to her for her son to follow suit.

"I heard she forgot to pick me up from the airport, with her irresponsible butt. I'ma kill her when I find her," D-Rock joked, but it wasn't contagious. JP shook his head in disgust. "Wha…what's up? She ok? Right?" D-Rock asked as his attention bounced from JP to his mom for assurance. He didn't like the chill that was elevating up his spine.

"Baby, have a seat. I have something to tell you…"

"No, I'm good standing up. Just tell me what happened. She ok?" His voice was beginning to shake. Yvette was his closest family member besides his mother. "Tell me…"

"Nigga she dead!" JP blurted as he hopped to his feet. His words paralyzed D-Rock. JP stepped in his face with a demonic look of pain. "Fucking dead! You understand what that means? That means she ain't never picking yo' sorry ass up from the airport, since that's what the fuck you seem to be worried about." JP stepped past him and bumped him hard with his shoulder. D-Rock snapped to his senses and followed his cousin out to the porch into the warm night air.

JP was holding on to a column as he just stared off into the distance, shaking his head with every memory that flashed in his recollection. "How?" D-Rock asked as he stuffed his hands in his pockets.

"Somebody cut her fucking throat. Right in her car…on her way home from work, my nigga," JP said as he faced his cousin. "Or have you forgot how shit go down here on this side of the world…you know the side you ran from? Shit was too hot and you got the fuck out the kitchen, so I bet this may even feel new to you, huh? Yeah, that's right. While you were out in Carolina eating BBQ and fucking white girls, Yvette was here getting burnt…in the fucking kitchen!" He paused and glanced over D-Rock's bruised face that was now low in shame. "The fuck happen to you anyway? You running from an ass whooping?" he asked. D-Rock touched the side of his face that was still a bit swollen from his bout with Brass and Wink.

"Oh, naw, I got into a car accident," he lied.

"Yeah, ok…" JP shook his head and pulled out a cigarette. As he lit it and took a deep inhale, he pointed at D-Rock. "So why are you here? You've been gone for years, and you just show up out of the blue…looking fucked up."

"It was just time for a change, man."

"Them Carolina niggas on your ass huh?" JP chuckled and took another drag. The setting didn't warrant jokes, but he needed to laugh even if it was forced.

"While you over there laughing, we need to be hitting these fucking streets trying to find out what happened to Yvette. Have you heard anything? Are the streets talking yet? Jealous ex-boyfriend? Something, nigga damn!"

"Nigga, it's only been six hours! Her blood still warm on these streets." JP pulled the cigarette.

"But, I heard a lil' something. Dunno how true it is since it's too damn early to tell."

D-Rock held his palms out ready for an answer that JP seemed to be beating around. "Well?"

"They say it was the Mexican Mafia."

"The Mexican Mafia? Why would they come at her? You serious?" D-Rock stepped closer.

"Baffles me too, that's why I didn't take it seriously."

"Well, shit, let's go…is that your truck?" D-Rock asked as he pointed.

"Yeah, where we going? You think you just gon' walk up on them niggas? You must be crazy! This ain't Carolina!"

Mama Rock stepped outside and approached D-Rock. She placed both hands on the side of his face and looked at him. "What happened to you Dante?" she asked in a worried tone.

"Oh, it was a car accident. I'm ok though." She squinted her eyes as she focused through his lies like all mothers could. "Don't worry, Mama, all of that is behind me. We'll be back," he said as he nodded towards JP. They hopped into his truck and peeled off.

~

They pulled up in front a beige house, and parked the truck. Immediately, figures stood up from the cluttered porch and stepped into the yard, hawking the unidentified and unwelcome vehicle. There had to be at least 10 shirtless Latinos on the porch and D-Rock counted five more scattered in the yard. All eyes were on him, and he could feel his heartbeat adjusting to the pressure. "You sure this is the spot?" D-Rock asked JP as he kept an eye on a short figure that was approaching the truck. His hand was tucked on his waist, gripping the butt of a pistol.

"Shit, don't it look like it?" JP commented. D-Rock sighed and pulled on the door handle. The dome light illuminated the car, and the short figure swayed his head side-to-side trying to recognize the occupants. "Aye, these chinos don't play that fuck shit, you hear me?" JP said as he grabbed D-Rock's arm. "I'm just warning you. Don't try to approach this situation like you back in Carolina."

"I got this. I'm just going to ask a few questions," D-Rock said.

"A'ight, the nigga you need to see is Chu-Chu. Don't worry about spotting him out the bunch. You'll know him when you see him." D-Rock pushed the door open and stepped out. The short figure hopped off the curb, still gripping his weapon and eying D-Rock and JP's movement.

"Aye, we are looking for uhhh...Chu-Chu..." D-Rock said, as he made sure to keep his hands in plain sight. The little guy cut his eyes at JP and then to D-Rock.

"The fuck for?" he asked aggressively. D-Rock looked over at JP. "Don't look at him, fucker! Keep your eyes on me. The fuck you need to speak to Chu-Chu about?" the little guy stepped in D-Rock's face and pulled the pistol out, letting it rest at his side.

"I just need to ask him about my cousin. She was murdered. I need to find out who did it...that's all man. No problems here." The little man squinted through his story just as Mama Rock did. He looked D-Rock up and down and walked a slow circle around him.

"So you think we had something to do with that? You here for revenge or sum?"

"No...but the streets are saying you did..."

"So what?" the little man hopped back in D-Rock's face and placed the gun under his chin. "What if we did? You a cop? You ready to die 'bout it?" D-Rock was scared shitless, but he refused to show it.

"Aye, we just wanna know if-" JP started but the little guy pointed the gun at him.

"Was I fucking speaking with you? Huh?" A group had migrated towards the scene. D-Rock watched the faces of malice and for a second he regretted the visit. Suddenly the group parted open and a tall prison built figure stepped through like a titan. He stepped forward and stood in front of D-Rock and JP. He wore a thick mustache, with tats covering 90% of his flesh. On his neck was the number 13, representing the 13th letter of the alphabet, 'M'. Mexican Mafia was inked all over his body, with a black hand in the center of his wide chest with an 'M' on the palm. On his shaved skull was a crow with a snake in its mouth, and blood leaking from its beak that trailed into teardrops under Chu-Chu's eyes.

"You must be talking about Yvette," he said as he crossed his arms. The small figure lowered his weapon and stepped to the side, keeping an eye on D-Rock. He was eager to bust his gun.

"Yeah, have you heard anything?"

"I heard somebody finally shut her fucking loud mouth." The crowd erupted into laughter. D-Rock and JP had to mask their anger with straight faces. "What? You didn't find that funny?" Chu-Chu asked as he stepped closer.

"I just want to know what happened...you know...for closure."

"Closure?" Chu-Chu looked back at the crowd. "Nah...I think you want blood. I think you heard it was one of us who did it. I think-"

"It's not lik-" D-Rock tried to stop him before he got the audience riled up.

"I think you came here thinking you were going to be this big gangsta hero and avenge her death...what do y'all think?" he asked the crowd. Nearly every soul pulled out a weapon of some sort and waited for the situation to escalade. D-Rock had to take a hard swallow. "Is that it?" Chu-Chu was now in D-Rock's face and could smell the fear dripping from his pores in the form of sweat. "I'm just fucking with cha!" he said as he playfully pushed him. D-Rock stumbled back as Chu-Chu and his crew broke out into laughter.

"So, you know who did it?" D-Rock asked as he cautiously walked back up.

"Why? I thought you were looking for closure..."

"Ok, or why she was killed?"

Chu-Chu chuckled. "Your cousin was living foul."

D-Rock looked at JP who shrugged in confusion as well. "How?"

"She worked at that shady immigration office..."

"Shady?" D-Rock raised a brow. "She loved that job, and was good at it, from what she told me. She did a lot for the community. A lot for your people might I add." D-Rock was hoping that last part didn't get taken the wrong way.

Chu-Chu and the crowd broke out into another gut piercing laughter. "She did a lot for the community! For my people? You must not be from around here!" JP lowered his head. "How about this..." Chu-Chu stepped closer. "She was murdered leaving her job, so I'd start there. I'm willing to bet my left nut that she tried to extort some poor immigrant," he paused and pointed at his chest. "My people, at that, and it backfired this time." He smiled as the confusion on D-Rock's face prevented him from receiving the true message. "Go see her boss, Cydney...speak with her, and you may find your answer."

"Her boss? She had something to do with it you think?" D-Rock questioned as Chu-Chu started to walk away with the crowd following his lead.

"I'd bet my other nut on that...that bitch is crazy, and would do anything to keep her shady little operation running smoothly...like any leader would," Chu-Chu spoke over his shoulder. "Just know, you won't find closure with that one, but you might see your cousin again sooner than later..."

My Hero

Death walked amongst the living and stole the joy from the souls around it. For the past week, the immigration department felt its presence as the workers grieved Yvette's untimely death. The laughter that made the hours fly by was gone causing their eight hour days to feel more like fifteen. Defectives swarmed throughout the building questioning all and subpoenaing the surveillance footage from Yvette's last day in the flesh.

Cydney hated to admit it but even she missed Yvette. She missed their daily spats and felt like a villain without a superhero. Killing Yvette had given her free range to move forward with her plan of stacking paper to fold, but it made it too easy and caused her to lose the thrill in her hustle.

"Cydney, baby, you haven't been out of this office all week. I'm dealing with the loss of Yvette but I don't know what I'd do if I lost you too. How are you holding up, baby?"

Ms. Stella slid into Cydney's office bringing the scent of mothballs and green rubbing alcohol with her. She was too old to pick up her feet and the heaviness of her orthopedic shoes weighed her down even more. She wore them for comfort, not giving a damn about being fashionable. She was a 63 years old widow and left looking good to the younger women around her.

"I'm holding up but sitting in Yvette's old office isn't helping me any."

"Well baby," she said finally making it to the seat across from Cydney. "I wanted to tell you before you heard it from anybody else. They think one of our clients had something to do with Yvette's murder. They say she refused to help a man who was getting deported and he waited for her to leave so he could follow her."

"Oh my God," Cydney's jaw dropped as she clutched the pearls that hung around her neck.

"Yes Lord. That's why I want you to know that I've requested early retirement. I was going to wait these two years out but my soul is telling me it's time to let go."

Cydney didn't say a word. There was something in Ms. Stella's face that said she wasn't finished talking.

"42 years...42 years I spent sitting behind that window. I've helped at least one person from each nation on God's green earth. Some thanked me and some cursed me out in their language from the sun and back. Luckily for them, I didn't know what they were saying or I would've dished it back," she laughed. "I've never been promoted and whenever I was asked to move up I declined. I wasn't about to volunteer for a new headache. I've lived life the safe way baby, never taking on any challenges unless it was for my kids. Now they're all grown and married with kids of their own. It's time I take being a grandmother as my fulltime role."

"I can understand that…" Cydney began but Ms. Stella held her hand up to shut her up.

"I'm not done, baby. I've known Yvette for eight long years. She started at the window next to me, was promoted to this here office, and was demoted back to my side. We talked at work and home but her conversations as of late had been solely about you. I think she had been talking about you for six months or…"

"About what?" Cydney cut her off trying to keep the old lady from rambling on like she tended to do.

"I said about you. You didn't hear me? Anyways, Yvette had her suspicions about you and the real reason you moved here from New York. I told her it was the devil whispering in her ear and she should pray on it but she wouldn't listen. Do you believe in God, baby?"

"Yes, I do but what does that have to do with what Yvette said about me? How about you get to the point, it's almost five." She couldn't hide the frustration in her voice even if she wanted to. Ms. Stella gave her a puzzling look but not one of questioning. The pieces of the puzzle Yvette were gathering had finally put themselves together and she realized she had already said too much.

"It wasn't anything important, baby. It's five minutes to five," she said using her hands to put her weight on the arms of the chair to get up.

"Sit your old ass down, Ms. Stella, and finish telling me what she said or I'll retire your ass today."

Ms. Stella's heart began tightening in her chest.

"Now tell me what she said." Cydney tried to sound like the sweet girl she knew Ms. Stella thought she was, but she could tell by the look on Ms. Stella's face it was too late for damage control.

"It wasn't important, Cydney. You know how Yvette's mouth…"

"Fuck that!" Cydney ran across the room and locked the door. She snatched Ms. Stella out of the chair by her buttoned up sweater. "What did the bitch say to you?"

"My heart," Ms. Stella said clutching her chest. "Baby, get my nitroglycerin off my desk."

"I'm not getting shit until you tell me." She released her sweater but the wrinkles from her grip remained balled up just below the neck.

"She thought you were doing illegal stuff, that's all. Now please, get my medicine."

With power building up from her frustration, Cydney punched her in her chest and Ms. Stella hit the floor unable to speak. Her heartbeat felt like there were a thousand knots tightening in her chest as her heart grew until the point it would pop. Cydney stood over her until she was certain death was near and then headed for the door.

"Somebody help, Ms. Stella is having a heart attack!" she yelled.

The office roared with concern and Cydney stepped out of the door for those making their way to help. One of the male detectives came running in past her to aid Ms. Stella as tears ran down Cydney's face. It only took a few failed attempts at resuscitation before the detective pronounced her dead.

Once the coroners left with Ms. Stella's body, pre-ruling her death as natural causes, Cydney called it a night.

"What a fucking day!" she yelled in the comfort of her car. She went from being questioned about Yvette's death all week to giving her eyewitness account of Ms. Stella's death. All she wanted to do at that point was ride in silence to her house and soak in her tub, but something in her rearview mirror caught her attention. She was being tailed two cars back by a pick-up truck. Whenever she turned right, it mirrored her action. When she suddenly switched lanes, it copycatted her move. She continued to play games in the interstates traffic as she watched the pickup truck follow her lead. Snatching her prepaid phone out of her purse, she called Tomas.

"Hey, I picked up a tail."

"The policia?"

"No, I don't think it's the police. Where are you?" she asked with her eyes locked on her rearview mirror.

"Collecting your money."

"Ok, I'll be there in five minutes."

She hung up and sat the phone on her lap just in case she needed to make a quick call and then headed towards her strip club. She didn't own it but she was on 90% of its strippers' payrolls. If you were beautiful with a banging body and wanted to stay in America, that's where Cydney would send you for employment. With the help of Tomas' staffing agency, on paper, the ladies were general laborers at a warehouse, but in reality, they swung from poles and did whatever else was necessary to give Cydney her $200.00 a day take.

It was Friday and after five, which meant the club would be packed with customers thirsty for the two for one drinks that happy hour furnished them. She passed up her normal employee parking spot and parked as a guest.

"I'm here, meet me at the door, but don't come out unless you see a reason to." Again, she ended her call with Tomas as fast as it had started. She lingered in her car to see if the doors of the silver F-150 would open, but they didn't, so she made her way out.

"Good evening Ms. Adore, I see you're using the guest entrance and not the employees. You must be here to relax," the goofy too big for his own good young black bouncer said but she ignored him, flying right past him.

"Where are they?" Tomas asked holding the inner doors open for her.

"They are in the silver F-150 parked by the light pole in the back. I'm going to have a drink at the bar. Keep your eyes on them."

Like Cydney had assumed, the club was packed and there wasn't a seat left at the bar, but she knew that would quickly change as she unbuttoned three buttons on her blouse revealing the line between her C-cups of birth given chocolate. She tied the long pearls around her neck in a knot that rested in between her breasts and snatched the clip out of her hair. Her naturally curly hair rested on her shoulders and she made her way to a group of black businessmen at the bar.

"Excuse me fellows but would one of you mind getting up so I can rest my feet?" she purred her words more than she asked them, and like magic, three stools were cleared. She selected the one in the middle to give her a good view of the club and shield her from onlookers coming in from the club's entrance.

"Can I buy you a drink beautiful?" one of the men standing around her offered as he slid his wedding ring off his finger, but Cydney was in a trance. The DJ was spinning hit after hit and put on a booty shaking old track by the Hot Boys. The dancers began popping harder and more of their already revealing clothing began to disappear. The entire club turned up a notch, which included the chants of the guests requesting the strippers take it all off.

"Nigga, look, her ass is so fat its dangling off the bar stool."

Cydney dug in her purse, pulled out a wooden Jamaican cigarette, and lit it up.

"If you don't seal the deal with that, I will."

She took two quick puffs while bobbing her head to the contagious rhythm.

"Are you going to make a move or what Mike?"

Her eyes watched as ones came pouring down like rain on the stripper that danced on the main stage.

"I did make a move. I asked if she wanted a drink but she didn't respond." He shrugged.

Looking from stage to stage a pale-yellow figure sitting alone in a dark corner caught her attention and she stood to her feet to approach it, but not before she directed her attention to the men holding a conversation about her like she wasn't there.

"Listen here, Mike. A woman likes a man that ain't scared to jump in the driver's seat and hit the gas. Instead of asking if you can by me a drink while I'm seated at the bar without one in my hand, you should've been asking me what I want to drink. Secondly, your ring should have been off before you stepped foot in here if you came with the intention of not leaving alone and that cheap ass cologne you're wearing is killing me. Now," she said focusing her attention on the tallest and oldest man in the group to add injury to her insults. "If he would have offered to buy me a drink, I would have immediately accepted it. Enjoy your visit fellas." She walked away with the childish taunts of the men behind her.

"Excuse the fuck out of me," she said to the Japanese girl who was sitting alone in the corner. "Why aren't you up on your feet dancing?"

Fear struck the girl's face at the sight of Cydney.

"I'm taking a break, I'm tired."

"Oh, I understand, that means you got my money?"

Kyoko had only been in American for a few months shy of a year and only planned to be there until she earned her degree. She had never experienced the evil Cydney was capable of, but she had heard the rumors.

"No, not yet. I've only been here two hours. I had class today, and I stayed up all night...." She searched for sympathy, but instead Cydney's hand came flying at her neck. With her thumb and index finger, she locked on Kyoko's thyroid gland and gave it a twist. Kyoko clenched expecting pain, but it never came. Where pain should have taken over, her body was filled with a discomforting beat that grew more in strength each second. The beat slowly took over her body causing her arms to jump in reflex. She could hear her breathing speed up from simply exhaling through her nose. Her body began to feel lighter and the dim lights in the club became brighter. Before her eyelashes could touch her skin, Cydney's grip was broken.

"You got two and they're seated at the far table to the right of us. Go to the second VIP room, it's empty. I want to see if they follow you."

Cydney pulled herself together and turned towards the VIP section after checking the two men out. She couldn't make out their faces under the dim lighting but their clothes said hip-hop, late 90's Jay-

Z era. Looking over her shoulder, she said, "I want my money before I leave."

The VIP rooms were small curtained platforms with their own stage. Each room could hold no more than 30 guests and four dancers at a time per the fire code. Unlike the other three rooms, the second housed an emergency exit giving Cydney a way out.

She debated transferring back to New York for months because the majority of the immigrants that came to her office were from Mexico and South American countries. They were hard people to break and the loyalty they shared amongst each other was hard to divide. It was easier in the big apple and less dangerous.

It seemed like every client's file that found its way on her desk, belonged to some distant relative of a member of the Mexican mafia. She wouldn't dare cross nor try to make extra money off them; they were off limits. She even took the extra step of questioning El Salvadorian Tomas if he had any family who was affiliated with the mafia and he assured her that if he did, he didn't know them.

Sitting in the room for ten minutes without word from either Tomas or the men who were following her had her ready to make the great escape. She could run out the door and head straight back to New York. She had enough legit money to restart her businesses in New York. In addition, with all the deaths in the Arizona office, she was sure the Department of Homeland Security would understand her emergency transfer.

"Just remember one thing, Cydney, get your money legally. Blood money always leaves a permanent stain." How she wished she had taken heed to her grandfather's words.

"Are you Cydney?"

The curtain opened and closed quickly but standing in front of her was a freshly battered man. He didn't look familiar and she couldn't place his accent, but could tell it was touched by the south.

"Yes, that's me. How can I help you?" Cydney said trying hard not to sound fearful.

D-Rock's eyes cased the room. There wasn't any music playing, the bar was closed, and the stage was empty. Cydney was sitting under very dim lights and he couldn't tell if she was holding a gun or a small handbag. Watching his eyes roam, Cydney saw him find comfort in the exit doors and decided to bring his anxiety of being in an unknown place back.

"Don't look so shocked, of course I was expecting to speak with you. You took the time to follow me here, why not setup an introduction. You know I'm Cydney but who the hell are you? Speak fast, this meeting will be short."

D-Rock stepped forward, hoping to get a better view. JP stood by the exit with his eyes on Cydney, but ears focused on the movement in the hallway beyond the curtains. "I want to ask you something, and I may come off a bit pushy, but it's something that I really need to know." He paused, hoping she'd guess his inquiry, but remained silent, forcing him to arrange his words carefully. Surely the beautiful woman in front of him couldn't possibly have anything to do with murder...she was killing those heels, but homicide? Not likely. "I'm trying to figure out why Yvette was killed. I... I just got into town a few days ago, and that's some fucked up news to be welcomed to. I asked around a bit and all fingers pointed towards you..."

Cydney stood up. "So, you're Yvette's cousin from North Carolina. We were supposed to pick you up last week but..." Cydney dug in deep until she could find the spot where sorrow lied. She was ready for her best actress of the year award. "But... she was killed." Cydney cried out with tears falling like a water facet. "Minding her own damn business, she was killed."

The curtain flew open like a flag caught in the wrath of a hurricane. Before JP could even react, Tomas punched him in the gut. When he hurled over for oxygen, an elbow landed on the back of his skull, sending him to his knees. He tried to gain his wits and grab the man's legs, but a sharp pain shot through his neck. JP reached for the wound, and felt the cold steel of a blade. He looked up at his killer and saw the rage in his eyes as Tomas twisted the blade. JP fell face first onto the carpet as blood sprouted from his neck until his heart stopped pumping it.

D-Rock turned around in shock, just in time to grab Tomas' wrist as he seized his neck. He tried to break the man's grip, but Tomas was far too strong. D-Rock immediately felt dizzy as the oxygen source to his brain was interrupted. His eyes watered, and knees began to buckle.

"I'm sorry D-Rock. I told you our meeting would be short."

With D-Rock secured in Tomas' arms, Cydney approached him. She checked his pants, ankles, and the small of his back, and he didn't have a gun.

"I think Yvette would be upset that you came this far to investigate her death and didn't bring a gun to avenge her. Is that how you all do it in North Carolina?"

Tomas tightened his hold around D-Rock's neck.

"Oh, I forgot you can't talk, I guess I'll talk and you listen. You want to know who killed your cousin," she said standing on her tippy toes in heels. "You came to find out if I know who did it, didn't you? Well..." she said with her lips softly touching his earlobe. "I killed her; I slit that bitch's throat."

As Cydney completed her sentence, the curtain opened.

*****

Kyoko adjusted her blonde low-cut wig and stepped out of the dressing room. She glanced around the club with her hands on her hips and initiated her hustle mode. She hated her job, and felt that it was beneath her station, but as an illegal immigrant, and compared to the jobs that her peers gotten upon arrival, the strip club was a blessing. All she needed to do was stick it out for a bit longer until she finished her degree, and then she'd be free of Cydney's debt...she hoped.

The club wasn't as packed as she preferred it, but out of the crowd of frequents, she noticed a table of new faces. They weren't dressed like they had a surplus of disposable income, but they'd be a start. She preyed on newcomers because they were green and uneducated to her prudish ways. She'd dance and give the allure that she was the type to go all the way behind closed curtains, like her peers, but she vowed to never let a John enter her precious canal.

"You boys need company?" she asked over the soft R&B tune in the background. JP looked up at her and shook his head no. She rolled her slanted eyes and sidestepped towards the next patron. "What about you? You scared like your friend here?" D-Rock tried to look around her thin frame and keep an eye on Cydney.

"Nah, we good," he said as he waved her away. Kyoko sucked her teeth and walked away.

"You do know you in strip club, right?" she asked nobody in particular. Across the room, she noticed another table of unfamiliar faces staring in her direction. One of the bigger characters smiled at her, and that was her signal. She licked her lips and leaned over their table, letting her large, obviously purchased, breasts entrap the criminal eye. "You spend money or you just here for AC like those clowns?" she asked in a seductive drawl.

Brass nudged Wink with a childish grin. In NC, it was very rare to see a woman of Asian descent, unless she was handing you a menu, let alone working in a tittie-bar- he could get used to AZ. Wink on the other hand was unmoved. He'd party once D-Rock's heart had officially stopped. Until then, he was going to stare a hole in the side of his head, marking the spot that he wanted to shoot. "Sorry, we good over here, ma'am," Reece said, not wanting to bring any more attention to their area than needed. They had followed D-Rock inside, and now they were just playing the waiting game. Hopefully, he'd dip off to the restroom unaccompanied, and make the task easy.

"Shit, speak for yourself!" Brass said as he dug into his pocket and pulled out a dollar bill. "You said blend in, right? We can't be the only niggas in here with no dancer," Brass reasoned.

"Chill, Brass. Remember why we are here," Reece mumbled to him. Brass ignored him and handed the bill to the girl.

"What can I get for that?" he asked as he rubbed his hands together like Birdman. Kyoko stared at the bill in disgust as she turned her back to them and started slow-winding. Brass watched her thin exotic hips through her leather red shorts as her cheeks seemed to glow under the lighting. He wanted nothing more than to shove his face in her shade, where the sun didn't shine. After about two minutes of a teasing routine, Kyoko turned back around and placed something on the table. They all looked at the item in confusion. She had folded the dollar bill up into an origami crane or some swan looking creature. She smiled as she stood up and turned to walk away.

"That's what dollar getcha…"

Brass had a face of embarrassment, but a nudge from Reece snapped him back into reality.

"Look, they are on the move," Reece said as he pointed at D-Rock. D-Rock stood up and walked through the door with his boy in tow. As the door swung shut, 'VIP' was painted on the wooden frame. An idea hit Reece. "Aye, excuse me," he said as he hopped to his feet and grabbed Kyoko's arm. She snatched it away in repulsion as she gave him the elevator eyes. "I'm sorry," Reece raised his palms in peace. He noticed two guards step forward from the other side of the room, so he dipped into his pocket and pulled out three hundred dollar bills. "We aren't from round here, so please forgive us, ok? Can we talk privately?"

Kyoko looked at the money and smiled. She already had enough to keep Cydney off of her ass. "Sure, follow me," she said. Reece signaled for his crew to follow. She led them through the door and into a small room. Before entering, Reece heard a familiar voice from the adjacent room and nodded towards it for Brass and Wink to check it out while he stalled the stripper.

"Your friends shy or something?" Kyoko asked when only Reece entered the room. He smiled and sat on the edge of the leather couch. She shrugged and started winding up for her routine but he stopped her with a slight grasp on her wrist. "What? Oh, don't tell me you're into that weird I Just Wanna Talk, shit," she said as she turned to him. Reece dug into his pocket and pulled out a

$100 bill. He needed to keep her distracted, and he figured he might as well get something out of it.

"That crane that you made back there," Reece started as he nodded over his shoulder. "You did that quick as hell. It normally takes me like 30 mins," he broke out into a chuckle. She just stared at him, shifting her eyes from the bill to his face, trying to get a sense of his gravity. "Can you teach me how to make them faster?"

"Dude, are you serious?" she asked as she stepped forward with her arms crossed. He smiled and made his eyebrows jump. "Ok, give it here. I'll do it for you," she said as she reached her hand out.

"No," he said. She looked up in confusion. "It doesn't count unless I make it." Just as he said that, he heard the commotion coming from the other room. Kyoko's jaw dropped as she picked up on his intellect to origami.

"You...you're trying to make the thousand?" she asked. Reece stood up, peeked out of the curtain, and smiled back at her.

"Yes...for Sadako..."

Brass and Wink pulled out their pistols and screwed on the silencers. They were in attack mode, and the previous immaturity had vanished from Brass' face. Brass stepped through the curtain and instantly saw his target being choked. That brought a smile to his face.

"Gotdamn, no sex in the champagne room for real though!" he said as he stepped over JP's body. "You Arizona folks are weird as fuck, feel me?" he said as he aimed his pistol at Tomas. Tomas was still holding D-Rock by his throat as Cydney ran to the corner of the room. Her heart was beating through her chest as she stared at the strangers with guns. "I'll be damned if I drove out here for nothing, let that bitch nigga go so I can finish what I started."

Tomas looked at the intruder and then to Cydney as he held the knife outward. She was in the corner acting scared, playing the innocent role like she was just a dancer caught in the wrong place. Wink stepped to the side with his pistol aimed at Tomas. Reece stepped in and observed the situation. He looked up at the ceiling for cameras and was relieved that he didn't find any. With a heavy sigh, he analyzed the situation and stuck his hands in his pockets.

"Who they?" Tomas asked Cydney. She didn't answer. She just stuck to her role; it was her only way out alive.

"Wink..." Reece said. Tomas looked at him. He seemed to be the man in charge, and the only relaxed soul in the room. "Kill him..." Before Tomas could duck, Wink pulled the trigger, sending a bullet right through his temple and flicking his off switch. The bass from the club muffled the silenced pistol fire. Tomas' body collapsed, D-Rock fell gasping for air, and Cydney fell in the corner, clutching her knees in fake tears of fright. Brass stood over D-Rock and smiled with Wink at his side.

"You fooled us twice, but you won't see a three, you understand?" D-Rock tried to raise his hands outward and plead for his life, but the strength in his body was depleted. "One..." Brass started to count. D-Rock looked over at his cousin who was sprawled out lifeless like a welcome mat near the entrance. He then looked over at Cydney. She was playing the game well. "Two..." He wanted to tell them that- POW! POW! Brass and Wink both patterned shots into D-Rock's skull. "Told you that you wouldn't see a three." Brass looked up at the girl in the corner and turned towards Reece. "Your call boss man..." Cydney looked up when he called him boss man.

Reece walked over to her and squatted before her.

"What is your name?" he asked.

"I didn't see shit, I didn't hear shit, and I don't know shit!" she blurted as she kept her face covered.

"Your name?" Reece repeated.

"I said, I didn't hear shit!" Cydney shouted. Reece smiled and stood up. He turned towards the door and walked past Brass and Wink.

"Leave her...she's a nobody."

"You sure?" Brass asked as he aimed his pistol. He wanted to shoot her anyway, just to send a message to Reece that he wasn't the one in charge, but he decided against it. He had got what he came for.

"Yeah, let's head back to Rock City..." Brass and Wink tucked their weapons. Wink exited the room behind Reece but Brass stalled. He waited for them to leave and walked over to the girl. He had to admit, she was fine, and he probably couldn't have pulled that trigger if he wanted to. He kneeled beside her and placed a hand on her shoulder. She flinched out of terror as she looked at him.

"Chill, baby girl. Listen though. If you're ever in NC and you want to escape this bullshit life that you are into, you should look me up." He made a fist and held it in front of her face, showing off his brass knuckles with the word 'Brass' etched into the business end. He watched her eyes as she read it and put together the pieces. He smiled as he blew her a kiss, and faded beyond the curtains.

Broken Bonds

The temperature of the bath water was perfect but the person occupying the watery space was far from it. The blood money Cydney had grown to love was leaving its stain. And it wouldn't take Maury to determine that the DNA in it could be traced back to her strain. Her mind wouldn't stop replaying the soon to be cold case she had witness three hours earlier. By the graces of the God, she no longer prayed to, she had made it out of the emergency exit and to her car before the killers from North Carolina could make it out of the strip club's doors. Or even worse, before they had a change of heart and decided to seal her fate as they had done Tomas.

Tomas, what will I do without Tomas? The thought wouldn't leave her mind nor did it provide her with answers. She had suffered an enormous casualty with the loss of Tomas. He was the plane that she piloted and all though she called the shots, it was Tomas's muscles that got the job done. Without his enforcement, her well thought out scheme was over.

The flow of water filled the tub to half of its capacity while the scented bath oils became one with bubble bath and grew into oily orbs. Once the froth covered her naked body to the chin, her silently released tears met it. In the mindset of the salty taste of the ocean her tears added flavor to her lips. She hated crying especially when the tears were caused from a loved one's death.

Cydney sank beneath the liquid to her own version of the lost city of Atlantis. She had discovered the hiding spot as a small child to escape from the cruelness of the world. She visited this happy space frequently and because of it, she was now able to hold her breath under water for sixty seconds at a time. Nothing could harm her there and she could clearly hear her own thoughts formulate without the interruptions of the world.

She came up to resupply her body with oxygen and then returned to her peaceful spot to plan her next moves. All tranquility was lost as she was met by Tomas' smiling face. Her mind was displaying the facial expression he had given her the most, and she was stuck with the image of his always smiling face. Shaking her head to erase the image she was snatched from under the water by her hair.

Blinded by the water and soapsuds that covered her face, she parted her lips to exhale. With no time allotted to seal them back a gun was placed in her mouth.

"What's up sexy?"

The voice belonged to a Mexican American that she prayed she would never encounter again, Tonto, Chu-Chu's right hand goon.

"So, you work for Disney now? You think you're a mermaid and shit?" He laughed at his own joke while wiping her eyes clear with his now free of her hair hand. She muffled a sound out of her mouth, vibrating the gun and he shoved it to the opening of her throat.

"Shut up, puta. You're killing my vibe." Tonto slowly moved the neck of the gun in and out of her mouth as he imagined it being the gun he had in his pants. "Oh baby…" he moaned gripping her hair again and forcing her to bob her head to his motion. "You like that shit, don't you? I knew you were a freak. A nasty girl, I like that."

He released her hair from the palm of his hand and folds of his finger so he could caress her skin. His fingers softly went down her neck like he was playing itsy bitsy spider with her nipples being his final destination.

"Damn you got some big ass nipples, sexy. Your tits look like Cadbury eggs and I'm that fucking bunny," he said as he pinched a nipple between the webbing of his fingers. He stopped

110

stroking the gun in her mouth and let it rest as he lowered his head to her breast. Roughly, he took her breast into his mouth and began sucking while she tried to pull away.

"Move again and I'll blow your wisdom teeth out the back of your fucking head. That's my chocolate nipple now, mermaid."

He was scaring the shit out of her literally and bubbles full of gas made their way to the top of the water to let him know.

"You're fucking nasty...say excuse me or some shit." He pulled the gun out of her mouth and pointed it at the center of her forehead.

"Tonto, that's enough. Bring Senorita Adore to me."

Chu-Chu didn't have to ask twice and he never did. Tonto placed the gun back in his waistline, picked her up out of the tub, and slammed her hard onto the black and white checked floor. Lucky for her, her head landed on Chu-Chu's white and black Nike Cortez.

Cydney didn't have a clue as to why any of this was happening to her. She broke her ass to make sure she never crossed Chu-Chu and his Mafia friends. She bent backwards to make them happy whenever one of their family members needed her help getting into America. *Had she denied access to one of his relatives*, she thought.

"I thought I told you never to cross me?"

"I didn't..."

A quick kick to her naked ass from Tonto shut her up. "Aye, this ain't the great debate. Don't say shit while Chu-Chu is talking."

The room fell silent accept for the sound of the water settling in the tub from Cydney being snatched out of it. Her heart knocked on her rib cage causing her lungs to speed up their movement. She knew Tonto meant business so she wouldn't speak out of line again.

"This shit is crazy," Chu-Chu said as he sat on the toilet upgrading it to his throne. "When my jungle fever having ass cousin told me the crazy God shit you were doing at the immigration office I told him not to fuck with you. I told him you couldn't be trusted and now look at him, dead at a fucking strip club that don't even have bad bitches in it." He laughed, Tonto laughed, but Cydney remained quiet. Tomas had lied to her about being related to the mafia and the thought of him lying to her, of all people, instantly broke her heart. "I think you know what happened to him too don't you?"

Cydney looked from Tonto to Chu-Chu waiting on the okay to speak, but quickly realized Chu-Chu was waiting for her answer his question.

"Yes, Yvette's cousin from North Carolina came looking for the guy who killed her and..."

"And you ratted my cousin out."

"No," she said replying to Chu-Chu's last words. "Tomas tried to protect me but there were more than two of them, but he did get one of them." Tears filled the banks of her eyes.

"I told you we should have killed those putos when they pulled up," Tonto words came out of his mouth without him thinking of the damage they would cause.

"Oh, so you think you should be the boss now, Tonto? You think you can call shots better than me?" Chu-Chu was now standing to his feet and less than an arm's reach from Tonto's face. Tonto had been over stepping boundaries into the land of disrespect as of late and Chu-Chu felt it was time to put him in his place.

"Hell naw, that's not what I was saying."

"It sounds like it to me," Chu-Chu countered.

"I was just sharing my thoughts, homes."

"So now I'm your fucking therapist? I don't need help from the village idiot; did you forget what your name means and why you got it?"

Tonto hated when Chu-Chu reminded him that he was all muscle and no brains. He didn't agree with him but pretending to made his life easier.

"Naw, I didn't forget."

"Your name means fool, vato. You think I should take the advice of a fool?"

As the men went back and forth on their power trip, Cydney took the opportunity to try and cover up. She crawled to grab a dry towel off the rack, and when her hand went up, two guns cocked.

"I like my dark meat without fat," Chu-Chu said pointing his gun at the spots on her body that housed a few extra pounds. "You don't have to cover that sloppy shit up. So...those two guys in the pickup truck had some other fools with them, how many?"

"Three others." She didn't have to think about it because all three had left an everlasting memory in her mind.

"Do you remember what those fools look like?"

She shook her head no not wanting to verbally lie.

"Come on, you think you're a boss bitch, freedom giving, God. You remember something."

"B.R.A.S.S, Brass. One of the guys had on rings made into brass knuckles that said Brass. The boss man called another Wink and they were from Rock City, North Carolina. That's all I know."

Chu-Chu looked into her eyes for the lies but he couldn't read them. The fear of having guns pointed at her and being naked in front of the two men made her eyes give off too many different emotions at once. Chu-Chu lowered his gun.

"Is that all you know?"

"Yes, that's it. I swear."

In a flash, Chu-Chu pulled out his pocketknife and stabbed her in the thigh. She screamed in pain until her falsetto voice turned into one of a bass singer.

"You swear but you lied. If that's all you know, then how did you know who the boss man was?"

She continued to scream and cry without answering Chu-Chu's question so he pushed the knife deeper into her flesh.

"FUCK! I knew he was the boss because the other two called him boss. They never said his name."

Without caution, he yanked the knife out of her thigh. "Okay but guess what? You belong to me now. If you want to live and keep your little operation at the immigration office going, you're going to help me find those fuckers."

"I don't know how to find them and my operation is over without Tomas."

"You want to live?" he yelled repointing his gun at her head.

She nodded her head yes.

"Then use that brain of yours to find those putos and I'll let you use my fool." He laughed, "Tonto will help with your God shit."

The men walked out as quietly as they had come.

*****

The drive back to NC was quiet as each occupant of the vehicle cycled personal thoughts and recants of recent events. Weed smoke polluted the interior of the rental. Reece wasn't an avid smoker like his peers, so he ended up catching a contact and fading into a slumber. When he woke back up, he was just in time to see the beautiful sign that welcomed them to Rock City. Wink was now driving, and Brass was stretched out in the backseat, snoring like a drunken bear.

Reece lowered his window and pulled out his cellphone. He had a few missed calls from DeAndrea, but that wasn't a priority. He needed to check in with the boss man, the real boss man, so he dialed Unc's number. The loud background on the other end gave away his location. "Yo, Unc. We made it back...can you hear me? Unc? Yeah, we just hit the city."

"Come to the game so I can get the run down in person," Unc said.

"Now?" Reece looked at his watch. It wasn't late, but the only thing that he had on his mind was a hot shower and his own bed- not particularly in that order.

"Yes, now," Unc said as he ended the call. Reece looked at the device in his hand and shook his head.

"Big man wants us to come by the school," Reece briefed Wink. Brass sat up and wiped his eyes as he looked around their setting.

"For what?" Brass asked in a raspy tone, catching the tail end of the conversation.

"Does it matter?" Reece shot at him. Wink pulled into the parking lot of Rock City High School and all three parties stretched their legs and popped their backs. It was written on their faces that they were depleted, but there was only one final step to the mission, and they could rest easy. They marched inside the school and found Unc sitting in his reserved section behind the coaches. His bench and the one behind him were vacant, giving him the needed privacy to discuss his business in public if need be. Reece hated meeting at the high school games, but Brass and Wink loved it. Wink enjoyed the sport, but Brass enjoyed the adolescent women. He made sure that he wore his two gold chains inside, hoping to catch the eye of somebody's daughter. Wink grabbed a box of popcorn and followed them to Unc's section.

"That was quick," Unc said as he leaned back and propped his foot on the back of the coach's chair. The place was packed, and the noise alone was giving Reece a headache. He massaged his temples as he sat beside Unc with Brass on the other side. "Everything work out?" Unc questioned, keeping his attention on the game.

"Yes sir. Smooth as honeymoon pussy," Reece answered. Unc chuckled and wrapped his arm around him.

"Can anybody place you clowns in the state?" Unc looked at him with a serious face that time.

"We good, Unc. Trust me," Reece answered.

"That's not what I asked…"

"Your boy is gone, so is his cousin that he had with him, and some Mexican," Brass threw in, wanting his voice to be heard.

"Nobody witnessed it go down?" Unc turned his attention to him. Brass held his words in his throat, wondering if he should tell the whole truth, and nothing but it…

"A stripper, but she won't say shit," Reece answered for him.

"And how do you know that? She saw y'all faces, right?"

"It was Reece's call…I said kill her…"

"Yeah, but she was terrified. She won't say shit. If anything, we helped her out and scared her out of that profession." Unc gave Reece a disappointed look. He reached into his breast pocket, pulled out a black handkerchief, and wiped the beads of sweat that congregated in the rolls of his neck.

"All I asked was for you clowns to make it clean, and you still made a mess." He shook his head and focused back on the game. "What about the Mexican?"

"What about him?" Brass asked wanting it to be known that it was he who took care of his side of things.

"We don't need any more problems, that's what, fool!" Unc snapped. "You think them Mexicans down there are like the ones here over in Sharpsburg? No! Those fuckers are connected. He could be tied to some gang or some shit. Now that's more problems that could've been avoided. You niggas should've caught D..." he paused and avoided speaking the name of a dead man. "You should've caught him by himself..." Reece and Brass stayed silent and gave Unc a chance to calm down. "Good work though...at least you got the rat-the pussy cat may become an issue. I just hope you niggas put the campfire out completely. I don't need Smokey the bear riding my ass again."

They watched the game in silence, other than chants and applause. Reece was ready to go home and was about to excuse himself, until Unc elbowed him for his attention. "You see that guy right there?" Unc asked as he pointed at a tall lanky figure running up the court. "That's a cash cow right there," Unc said as he smiled at him. "He's my ticket out. See, I do think long term. Like you said, this drug game isn't forever...I see that now," Unc said as he rubbed his large hands in anticipation.

"You're going about it wrong, Unc," Reece said. He was happy that he was finally coming around and seeing the future for what it was, but he still had the dope boy's mentality.

"What do you mean? He's a sure bet. In a few years he'll be in the NBA, no doubt about that."

"Yeah, but there's a better way to do it..." Unc shot to his feet in cheer as the player caught an awkward angled Alley Hoop and slammed it in. He winked at Reece and pointed to the player as he sat back down.

"Do tell, advisor."

"See, you're thinking you can invest some money in him, use your pull, and get him to the big leagues. Then he will get that check and pay you back with interest."

"Exactly..."

"But it doesn't work like that. That's how you end up like Chris Webber and the Fab 5...you gotta be smarter about that shit nowadays, Unc." Unc turned and gave him his undivided attention. "Listen," Reece started as he leaned closer, reading the confusion on Unc's face. "You have to invest in this kid, but also invest in a business. That way when he makes it, instead of cutting you a suspicious check, he just in-turn invests in your already lucrative business...he gets his teammates involved as well, and bam!" Reece punched his palm; he was awake now. "Unc's Chicken and Ribs is a fucking success." Unc smiled and leaned back.

"Is that your plan? Start a rib joint?" Unc asked showing all of his teeth.

"No...I'm still mapping that part out." Unc nodded and tapped Brass. He had to nearly slap his arm again to get his attention from flirting with the wide-eyed junior behind them.

"My bad, what's up?" Unc stared at him for a second to transmit his thoughts telepathically.

"Listen, go to...aye Reece, lean over here and listen up, you too Wink-a-Dink," Unc signaled. "Go see Seymour and pick up some cash for me. Should be about 400 large." Brass' eyes nearly fell out of their sockets like sleeping yo-yos. "420 to be exact. Take 100 of it, and divided between you and Bullwinkle over there." Wink smiled, not at the money, but whenever Unc joked with him, he knew that he was pleased with his efforts. "Drop a hundred at the spot for me to pick up later, and take the rest and drop it off at Reece's crib, tonight..."

"Tonight?" Reece asked as he looked at the time on his phone.

"Yeah, unless you got something better to do?" Reece powered on his phone when he saw a message from DeAndrea come through.

"Nah…"

"Ok, then you will take that 220, send 20 to D-Rock's mother, you understand?" Reece nodded. "Take your 50 out, how much does that leave? 150?" Reece nodded. Brass counted on his knuckles. "I want you to hold on to the rest…look at it…smell it…taste the blood on it, and in a few days we will go over your plans for this business venture. Are you up for that?" Reece nodded and stood to his feet. "Good…a few days, Reece. If you don't have any good ideas by then, then I want my money back…with interest for wasting my time and getting my hopes up, ya dig?" Reece nodded and patted Unc's shoulder as he turned to exit. Brass and Wink stood up to follow him. "Oh and boys, good work out there," Unc said as he turned and focused on his other team that he was coaching. Same game…different players…

*****

When Reece got home, he showered and flopped across his bed, shirtless with a pair of basketball shorts on. He forced his eyes closed, but his thoughts kept the sandman at bay. His chance was finally upon him; his chance to step out of the drug game and enter a legitimate business opportunity. It had taken him years to finally convince Unc to make the transition. He guessed that since Unc was getting up in age, and the last prison threat was still a tender wound, now was about the best chance for him to capitalize on it.

He rolled over to his back and stared at the ceiling. As hard as he squeezed, his eyes just wouldn't stay shut. He needed a plan, and Unc had only given him a few days to come up with something solid...but what? He closed his eyes and had a flashback to the strip club in Arizona. There was surely some dirty money on spin-cycle in that establishment, but would that avenue work in a small town such as Rock City? His thoughts haunted him. He had an idea on the tip of his tongue, or maybe it was a swollen taste bud of greed...or maybe it was a lie bump...

How can I make something out of this money?

The image of the Asian girl with the origami dollar blinked in his head, but he couldn't make sense of it. He needed to relax, so he hopped up and went to the fridge. He grabbed a few beers and placed them on the coffee table as he turned on his entertainment center. As he cracked open a beer, he lounged on the sofa and grabbed his X-Box One controller.

From the time he graduated college, he and a few friends kept in touch by playing online video games- *Call of Duty* mostly. They'd link up on Friday or Saturday nights, whenever Reece was free, and spend hours reminiscing and clowning on each other. They all took separate lanes in life after college, but Reece was the oddest ball out of the bunch. His peers had taken their degrees and landed jobs at big fortune 500 companies in Raleigh and Charlotte, while Reece went home and played sidekick to a kingpin. Same game...different players...

"Well, well, well, look who finally got his ass online." Reece grabbed his headset as his friends started in on him. They took *Call of Duty* seriously, because that was the only action that they got to see in their mundane lives. Reece on the other hand saw war every day. Hell, he had just gotten home from a deployment, it seemed.

"Don't start your shit, Chris. Unlike you slackers I had to work all weekend," Reece countered as he took a sip of his brew.

"Work? And where is it that you work, Reece?"

"Yeah, 'cause you looking like Tommy from Martin right now, homie!"

"You ain't *got* no job, nigga!" They continued to rag.

Reece had to laugh at their performance. "Whatever, niggas. I just got back from Arizona. Business trip…"

"Arizona? The fuck for?" Chris asked.

"Are you a drug dealer?" Don asked in a comical tone.

"If I was, I damn sure wouldn't tell you corporate rats!"

"Nigga, kill that noise! What, you think the feds listening to X-Box Live? Fuck outta here!" Don fired.

"Aye, Reece, real talk…" the airwaves got quiet. Reece knew that his friends cared about his wellbeing, but he could never let them too close to his troubled life. Maybe once he got his business, whatever that was, off the ground, he'd stunt on them with the news. "If you need a few dollars till Friday, just-" Chris couldn't stay in role from bursting out in laughter. "Just let us know, my nigga! I'll wire you $20 so you can buy some food stamps, or something!" Chris and Don erupted in laughter and Reece had to sit there and take, all in good sport of course.

"Say what you will, but I just made 50 large…this weekend. That's more than half of your salary from kissing ass, my G…" The airwaves got quiet again. "Like I thought, now gon' head and start the match, damn!" After a few beers, and tons of jokes being traded, Reece was feeling himself, just slightly. His doorbell ringing caught him off guard. He walked over to it with the headset still on, thinking that it was Brass dropping off his cash, but it wasn't. As Reece opened the door, her perfume preceded her. He had to blink a few times to make sure that his eyes weren't playing tricks on him.

"DeAndrea, what do you want?" She let her tipsy eyes trace his torso down to the bulge in his shorts as she licked her lips. She had to lean on the door to keep from falling over.

"Fuck you mean what do I want? I haven't heard from you all weekend, and you...and you got the balls to ask me that?" She reached for his balls but he swatted her hand. "Why I gotta hear from other niggas that you made it back safely?" Reece knew she was drunk. He also knew that Brass could swing by any minute, and it wouldn't be a good look if he caught her there.

"Yo, Reece, who that? She sounds sexy than a muhterfucka!"

"Probably a hooker. That nigga lame like you when it comes to pussy. Y'all never could close deals," Chris fired at Don from the headset.

"Nigga...WHO AIN'T GOT NO BITCHES?" Don responded, mocking the old internet sensation. Reece felt himself about to laugh so he muted the mic and removed the headset.

"D, you gotta go. Brass on his way, do yo' drunk ass understand?" Reece said sternly as he pointed past her. She ignored his warning and stepped forward, slamming the door behind her. Her heels exaggerated her height, making it possible for her to stand eye to eye with him, even though hers were heavy and reddened with alcohol.

"I'll tell you what I understand. I understand that you aren't taking this thing of ours seriously. Maybe Brass does need to catch us. Maybe that's the only way your timid ass will man up and tell Unc about us." She stepped closer with every syllable until Reece was backed up against his counter...he placed his palms on the marble to brace himself from falling and accidently knocked over a bottle of aspirin. It tumbled into the sink, breaking the awkward silence in the room but DeAndrea never broke her stare.

"You're fucking crazy. We don't have shit, you understand? You're going to fuck around and get both of us killed. In fact, this shit is over..." Reece thought his words would sober her up, but it was like another shot to her kidney. She smiled and slid her fingertips down his bare chest. His dick wasn't on the same page as his mind, so it stood out like a sore thumb...hitchhiking for her lips to lift a nut right out of it. She smiled and dropped to her knees. "D...Stop...You hear me? St..." The warmth from her lips was like a drug entering his vein, tranquilizing his soul. He gripped the counter tighter as she went to work, clutching his balls in her palm while driving his stick shift insane, never stalling once.

Reece tried to fight back, but it was pointless, he'd have to break it off with her later, right now-he just wants-he just wanted to-to… "Fuck it, I'm cumming!" he shouted as he grabbed the back of her head and jammed his shaft further down her throat. He gasped, but moaned out of delight as his warm fluids coated her throat. She held his dick in the position, swallowing and squeezing the muscles of her throat every time his dick pulsed and dripped aftershocks of semen. Slowly she slid back and observed his now limp rod. She loved bringing him to his knees, especially when he thought that it was the other way around. He was still gripping the counter like Jack on the door in *Titanic*. She just looked at him, wiped her mouth, and stood to her feet.

"Call me tomorrow. We will go over my plan to get rid of this extra baggage…you understand?" she taunted as she opened the door. She froze in her steps at the threshold.

Reece was still paralyzed but got control of his body when he felt the draft from outside hit his sweaty skin. He looked over and saw D standing in shock at the doorway, standing in front of her was

Brass. "Excuse me," she said as she fixed her face and stepped past him. Reece quickly pulled his shorts up and tried to erase the guilt from his face, but it was too late. Brass watched as D pulled out of the driveway in her convertible and then turned to Reece with a forced smile on his face. He tossed the duffle back at Reece's feet and then gave him a serious look.

"This can go down three ways, Reece," Brass started.

"Brass, listen…"

"Nigga, shut the fuck up! You not about to hit me with that it's not what it looks like bullshit! Ok?" Reece nodded in defeat. "Now like I was fucking saying, it can go down three ways. One, you can man-up and tell Unc; hopefully he'll put a bullet in your head. Two, I can tell him, and hopefully he'll reward me by letting me put a bullet in your head or…" Brass reached in his back pocket, pulled out a pack of cigarettes, and lit one up as he mugged Reece. "Three, you can just disappear. Pack yo' shit, move to Arizona, or some shit. Kill that noise about going legit and leave this hustle to me. You understand?" Reece just stared at him. He couldn't believe he had allowed himself to get caught up and now Brass had the upper hand. "My nigga, I need to hear that you understand, or I might as well kill you right fucking here," Brass said as he stepped closer. His brass knuckles gleamed under the porch light as he tightened his fist at his side.

"I need some time, Brass," Reece said as he lowered his head. Brass was enjoying seeing defeat on his nemesis' face.

"I'll give you a few days, like Unc did," Brass said as he reached into the duffle bag and pulled out a few stacks of the money. He held it up and smiled at Reece. "I'm taking this from your cut as a penalty," he said as he walked back towards his vehicle. Reece squinted to see if Wink was inside and now hip to his secret as well, but Brass must've dropped him off prior. "See what pussy get you?" Brass asked as he waved the stack of money out the window and pulled off.

Reece slammed the door with rage flowing through his veins. He could choke D for the stunt that she had just pulled. Her drunk ass didn't even know the shit she had just stirred. Reece turned on the water in the sink and grabbed the pill bottle. He gripped the wet lid and finally got it off as he pinched two pills out. He cupped his hand under the faucet and brought it to his mouth as he swallowed the pills. Then he put both hands under the stream and splashed the cool water over his face. He turned off the faucet and leaned back against this sink with his arms crossed as the liquid dropped from his chin and cascaded down his chest. He had to outsmart Brass, or come up with his own option four…

Reece shook his head and exited the kitchen. The headset was still on the counter of the crime scene.

"Yo, Reece…you straight?"

 Big Daddy

Sleeping had become a foreign act in the days that followed Cydney's partnership with Chu-Chu. Even the pain medications she received from the hospital for the stitched wound in her thigh weren't strong enough to let her close her eyes. Day and night, her hunt for the men from North Carolina ran non-stop. While at work, she used different search engines to read articles of violent acts in Rock City but none mentioned the names that circulated through her head. Brass... Wink... boss man...were ghosts in their city. If they were pulling moves like they had done in Arizona, then she applauded them for mastering the art of killing by shadow.

"Maybe they were small time," she said aloud but her mind thought differently. Her heart even pumped differently as she felt the veins in her wrist jump with every stroke of the computer keys. They lived in the age of the internet and almost everyone on the planet was Google-able to a certain extent. If she couldn't find a trace of the men on the World Wide Web, than how in fuck would she be able to track them down in a state she knew nothing about?

She reached for the flask in her purse and took a swig while ducked under her desk. If it weren't for the smooth burn of the brown liquor keeping her emotions at bay, she'd be crazy.

"Hey lady, you want anything from the…"

Getting caught drinking on the job was bad, but being caught by her supervisor could mean death to her career.

"Cydney, what are you doing?" the short balding older white man asked hurriedly closing and locking the door behind him.

"Exactly what it looks like, Mark. I'm taking a shot to ease my nerves. I keep seeing Ms. Stella die, right there, in that exact spot you're standing in. And Yvette…" she said turning up her flask again at the sound of her name.

"Now Cydney we could have pretended that I didn't see the first sip but for you to do it again…" He walked over to Cydney and placed a hand on her shoulder. "I know it's been hard." Slowly, he removed his hand from her shoulder like a credit card being swiped after a bad reading. "If I didn't have to be here right now, I'd use my vacation and sick days, but you don't have to be here…"

Cydney waited for him to continue and once she realized an annoying silence began to build, she looked up at him. He held a flask monogramed with M.T. to his lips.

"Pack your desk; I'm putting you on family medical leave with mandatory therapy. I know you were close to both ladies and this office isn't where you need to be right now. I'll swap offices with you when you return."

She remained silent as she began shutting down her computer to show she was listening. His hand fell back on her shoulder.

"Take as much time as you need but when you return make sure you leave your flask at home." He gave her shoulder a squeeze. "If you need someone to talk to, I'm here."

She locked eyes with him and saw the lust in his. He wanted her and he made that clear whenever he had the opportunity to. Mark wasn't hurting to the eyes but he was short and there was no way his five foot one inch frame was going to get in between her thighs. It didn't matter to her that he was her superior but the image of her wrapping herself around him and watching him disappear in her love was a turn off.

"Thank you, Mark," she said standing to her feet. When they were face to face, she reached in and kissed him. Not soft and romantically but one of those kisses that would lead to clothes being snatched off and her legs extending to the air. Her tongue slapped against his seconds before she sucked on it like a *Now and Later* forcing it to the roof of her mouth. Just when the mood was getting good, she snatched away, unlocked her office door, and said, "I look forward to seeing you when I return." She strongly believed in keeping an Ace in her pocket.

****

The coffee shop was packed which was strange to Cydney seeing it was mid-summer, but she understood the year around cravings for Joe. Melrose Coffee shop was the only establishment where Cydney had the patience to wait in line but the young guy behind her was making it hard for her to wait that day.

"You don't have to pay for it Ma, you can have it for free as long as you share my demo with your friends. I'm just trying to spark a buzz in my city right now."

She snatched the CD out of his hands and turned her back to him.

"And if you're on Facebook or Instagram you can follow my struggle to the top on them. People say I'm the next Kendrick Lamar."

It took everything in her not to turn around and say, "The industry isn't looking for the next Kendrick, it's looking for the next lyricist that's going to shut him down." But why kill the young man's dreams?

After a ten minute wait she was out of the coffee shop and getting in her car. She threw the CD on her lap vowing to give it to the first guy she saw sagging and put the key in the ignition. She wouldn't dare throw her car in drive without first taking a sip of her iced coffee. The way the mocha slid across the ice making for the chilled taste on her tongue was heaven on earth. Her guilty pleasure was interrupted by her cell ringing.

"Hello?"

"What's up mermaid, any news on those vatos?" Tonto asked.

She hadn't spoken to him or Chu-Chu in two days. A part of her hoped they had terminated the agreement and that they would find the guys on their own.

"No, not yet but..."

Her eyes had seen the light so to speak. It was as if her vision had instantly gotten ten times clearer as she stared at the social media sticker on the CD case. She had searched the internet but she hadn't searched the social media outlets.

"I maybe on to something, can you call me back in two days?"

"Aye, you need to treat this shit like that hour glass on *Days of our Lives*. You're running out of time, mermaid. Once that sand hits the bottom,

I'm going to fuck you in that big ass tub of yours and then drown you in it. You got two days."

The call ended and she quickly went through her contacts and sent the call. "Kyoko, I need your help with something. Where are you?"

If anyone knew the ins and outs of social media, Kyoko was the one. She had deemed herself queen of the selfie on Instagram after every performance on the main stage. Cydney didn't know if Instagram worked like Facebook, but it didn't hurt to try.

"You got to make an account first." Kyoko said logging out of her account.

"I don't want an account. I just want to search for some people, you can't use yours?"

Kyoko popped her gum several times in a row before answering. "I can use mine," she said logging back in. "But if you need to add them as a friend you have to make your own page. I only use Facebook for my fans."

Fans? Who does this Japanese bitch think she is, Beyoncé? Cydney thought it but wouldn't dare say it because she needed the help.

"Where do they live and what's the name? I hope you're not trying to catfish nobody."

"Catfish?"

"Never mind, I forgot you were too old...I mean too busy running your business to get on the book." She quickly recanted her previous statement.

"The name is Wink and he's in North Carolina."

"Spell it and what part?"

"Rock City, North Carolina and I think it's W.I.N.K."

"Is the city's real name Rock City?"

It hadn't been five minutes and Cydney found herself getting agitated by all the questions combined with Kyoko's accent.

"I don't fucking know if it's the real name of the city or not. Can't you just look, damn." She snatched the flask out of her purse and took a sip.

"Chill out, you don't have to get worked up. The queen of the selfie got you covered, honey."

Kyoko started searching and typing away. After moments of focusing on her MacBook, she looked up at Cydney.

"No Wink, who else you got?" The popping of her gum had gotten louder.

"Try Brass, it might be spelled like an acronym."

"Nope, who else you got?" She popped her gum again.

"Did you try to spell it regularly and stop popping that damn gum for I pop you!"

Kyoko swallowed the gum hard and started back typing.

"There are 15 Brass. You see his picture?" She turned the MacBook toward Cydney and slowly scrolled down the search results. It wasn't until they reached number 14 that Cydney had found her man. Brass' display picture was the exact replica of her last encounter with him, a balled fist displaying the word Brass spelled across his fingers on brass knuckles.

"How do I talk to him on here?"

Kyoko exhaled loudly.

"What you want to say? I can send him a message."

"Tell him that I'm coming to North Carolina and I want to see him."

"You sound thirsty. Let me show you how to get your man."

Kyoko clicked on a button that read poke and then pulled out her cell phone. She scrolled through her apps until she found what she was looking for and selected it. Rhianna's voice came blaring through the small speaker on her phone. She was singing about giving someone a round of applause. Cydney had heard the song before, but never knew the lyrics until Kyoko grabbed her hairbrush, and began singing along with her. Once the song went off, the next track played, followed by *Diva* by Beyoncé. The hook only played shortly before her MacBook made a strange sound.

"You see, he poked me back. Now watch this." She ran her fingers across the keys writing,

"What's good daddy? Can I call you sometime?"

When she hit send, she stood up and started dancing to the beat. Cydney had watched Kyoko strip at least a hundred times and it always shocked her to see Kyoko's skinny, large breasted body move better than most black girls.

"Are they real?" Cydney asked.

"I paid for them," Kyoko said raising her shirt and freeing her breasts from the restraints of her bra. "They were the first thing I brought when I came to America." Kyoko put her breasts in Cydney's face.

"Feel them."

With hesitation, Cydney grabbed them. She couldn't believe how natural they felt. With one hand holding Kyoko's right breast, she reached under her shirt and grabbed her own. The likeness was surreal.

"It's saline, not silicone. I'm a woman not a plastic Barbie doll." Kyoko laughed as her MacBook made another sound.

"Hell yeah, baby, 252-555-5555 call me now," Brass wrote back.

"There goes the number. Anything else?" Kyoko asked.

"Yes, let me use your cell phone."

She handed it to her against her will.

"Hello, can I speak to Brass, please?"

"This him. Is this that sexy Asian piece?" A voice in his background screamed, "Put it on speakerphone, my nigga."

"No sexy, I'm prettier than that," Cydney said feeling slightly childish at the game she was playing.

"Damn, Brass. Who's that?" the voice in the background asked.

"One of my hos nigga, shut up," he answered before speaking back into the phone. "You're sexier than that? Damn, who is this?"

"Guess."

"Come on now baby, daddy ain't got time for all that, tell me."

"Well, you said if I'm ever in North Carolina to look you up."

Brass fell silent for a second and then came the sound of him fumbling with his phone. When he spoke again, his phone was no longer on speaker.

"Hold on for a second beautiful." He placed his hand over the receiver before speaking to his boy.

"I gotta take this call; I'll get you with you later. Don't say shit about what I told you about that nigga Reece. I'm not ready to tell Unc about his bitch ass yet."

Cydney grabbed a pen off the desk and wrote, "Reece? Unc?"

"What's good with you Arizona? You in my city?"

"No, but I'll be there some time tomorrow. Will you be my tour guide?"

"Hell yeah I will. What brings you to Rock City?"

Cydney hadn't thought out her plan that far but it was nothing to come up with a lie. "My job is thinking about transferring me there to take over operations and…" she said adding the feel of horny to her voice. "And you've been on my mind since I met you. I want to feel how hard your Brass gets."

Up until then, Kyoko sat quietly swiveling her chair left to right but at the sound of Cydney's last words, she cheered her on with a high five.

"Get yo' man, girlfriend."

"Who's that?" Brass asked quickly.

"Oh, that's my homegirl from the strip club. I'm chilling at her house right now."

"Oh, ok. Shit, you sure you can handle my brass? A lot of women have asked for it but can't handle it when I give it to them. Big daddy don't play no games if you know what I mean."

"Big daddy, huh?" Cydney laughed at the nickname he gave his Johnson. "Well me and big daddy will just have to meet up and see what happens then. Do you know where I can get a five star hotel at the last minute? I'll only be in town two days and one night?" she cooed into the phone.

"There's always vacancies at Chez' Brass. Yeah baby this thug knows a little French but if you're only in town for one night, you can stay at my spot."

"But, I'm not coming alone. My girl Kyoko or the queen of IG is coming with me." Kyoko shook her head no but Cydney overlooked her. "I wouldn't want to intrude on your personal space."

"The more the merrier, baby...Aw shit, that's that little Asian bitch I met. Hell yeah, bring that bitch with you."

"Bitch?" Cydney said with attitude in her voice.

"Come on, baby, I said bitch for lack of a better word. I know how to talk to hos...I mean women. If she's your friend, she's my friend too." Nasty thoughts of big daddy in and around both women's mouths grew a smile on his lips.

"Are you sure? Do you think you can hook her up with that Bossman guy that was with you?" she threw the bait and he bit it.

"You talking about Reece? That nigga ain't the boss of shit, I'm the boss, and he's a faggot. He don't do pussy."

She wrote boss man next to Reece's name on the paper.

"My boy Wink will show her a good time while she's here. Don't worry about shit, baby, just get here, and call me. I'll even show you a little southern hospitality and pick y'all sexy asses up from the airport. Hit me when y'all touch down." He hung up and she handed Kyoko her phone back.

"I'm not going to North Carolina with you to meet some guys," Kyoko said putting her foot down.

"You will go and do whatever the fuck I tell you to do or you can earn your degree outside of the United States. Plus, these niggas are ballers. I bet my life you can make a years' worth of tuition in one night with these niggas." Cydney fed her the lie to ease her nerves.

"They big ballers like *Forbes* list or *Love and Hip Hop Atlanta*?" Kyoko asked while placing another piece of gum in her mouth and popping away at it.

Cydney didn't pay her attention. She was too busy searching for red eye flights so that they could leave that night. Once she downloaded their e-tickets, she slapped Kyoko across her face and the gum flew out of her mouth.

"Pack your shit, I'll be back to pick you up in an hour."

# Road kill

The airport was a scary place to sleep overnight. No matter how Cydney propped the bag under her head, there was something about the silver poles draped in black leather on the chair that wouldn't allow her to slumber. Not to mention the fact that she was on her way to see a murderer. She watched the airport janitors and employees walk the floor until the sun lit the room through the movie screen size windows. Their layover was in Nashville and although they offered her a hotel room; she didn't want to miss her 6 am flight. The plan was to get to North Carolina, check in to a hotel, swing back to the airport, and then call Brass. She didn't trust him enough not to have some form of security blanket set up. She even called Chu-Chu to inform him of her plan. If she told him what he needed to know, he was headed her way.

The flight from Nashville was short and to her surprise, there was a Marriott shuttle already waiting for guests outside. They unpacked and got ready. Cydney knew they thought she was a stripper so she threw on a tight white low cut top and a high-waist ankle-length jean skirt to hide the healing stab wound in her thigh. Now that she walked with a slight limp, she felt every bit like the mermaid Tonto nicknamed her. Kyoko had on a lime green, pleated shirt outfit, and white and lime green low cut tennis shoes to match. If the shuttle driver had driven any slower, Brass would have caught them exiting it.

"What's up ladies, I'm Brass and this my boy Wink. Y'all got y'all's bags and shit?"

Cydney didn't say a word. She grabbed her bag, smiled, and shook it. "Cool, just throw y'all shit in the trunk and get in." Brass was back in the driver's seat before Cydney could force him to be a gentleman. "So what y'all trying to do first, y'all hungry?"

"No," Cydney said with too much on it. "I want to relax for a second; can we go straight to your house? I'll look up a restaurant once we get there."

"The Waffle House stays open all day and night baby, you don't have to worry. I'll feed you."

"I didn't come all the way from Arizona for Waffle House," Kyoko said snatching her headphones off her ears. "I'll feed myself. I'm not eating Waffle House." She leaned closer to Cydney and whispered, "I thought you said they were ballas?"

It took longer than she had expected to get to Brass' house. She had kept up with the turns he was making until he went up a hill. When he came down the cement roads where gone and replaced with dirt. The buildings and streetlights had turned into a wall of beautiful trees and 'Caution Deer' signs. The sight was beautiful but fear was kicking in. She lowered her window to get a whiff of fresh air and was hit with something purer. The air was sweet and lacked the roughish feel to it. In an instant, her anxiety was gone. She was ready to play the game.

"Sorry about that long ass ride but we're here now," he said looking at the goofy smile Wink had on his face. If he hadn't known Wink all his life, he would have thought he was about to get his first piece of pussy by the excitement in his eyes.

They turned into the driveway of a nice suburban home. Judging from the outside, Cydney thought it could have been two or three bedrooms. The men hopped out and led the way into the house. At first glance, Cydney could tell that Wink and Brass lived together because the family style home had been turned into a huge bachelor pad. There were four leather beanbag chairs tossed around the living room and a 92-inch television set in the center blocking a window. You would have thought he had kids by the piles of video games and DVD's that covered the floor. There were game controllers and headsets hooked to the walls. If it weren't for them and the rap version of the Lord's last supper with Tupac and a few others in it, the walls would be bare.

"Welcome to our spot ladies, make yourselves at home. The first bedroom is mine and the one in the back is Wink's. The bathroom in the hallway is broken so y'all got to use the one in my room. This first time home owning shit is fucking me up."

"I'm going to the restroom, excuse me." Cydney dashed through Brass' surprisingly clean room and went into the bathroom. She missed the name of the street on the street sign but thankfully, it was written on his mailbox. She locked the address into her phone and then rolled her eyes at the roll of toilet tissue lying on its side on the floor.
Cydney returned to the living room but Wink and Kyoko were gone. He had taken her to his room to try and get a quickie in before they headed back out the door.

"You looking good baby, turn around for daddy." Cydney began to circle around slowly. "You got a little booty on you too but you make up for it up top." Brass walked up to her and rubbed his hardness across her ass. "That's all brass right there baby."

"So I was thinking you should pick the restaurant, but somewhere really nice." Cydney had turned all the way around and flopped down on to a beanbag. Her weight made it feel like she was sitting on the floor.

"I know a little spot we can go to. Let me change my clothes and get that nigga Wink."

Brass didn't have a spot but Reece did. He used to brag to Unc about taking all his dates to a small Italian spot. He had never eaten there, but if it was good enough for that lame ass nigga, he'd give it a try.

"Told you I know how to treat a lady, this shit nice. Ain't it?" Brass said showing all his off-white teeth as they arrived at the restaurant.

"Isn't it, please say isn't it. You're killing me with saying, ain't it," Kyoko said shrugging her shoulders in disgust.

"I keep telling him..." Reece had walked in behind them so he couldn't make out the ladies' faces, but once he began to pass them, he realized exactly who they were. "What the fuck y'all niggas got going on?" Reece asked stepping to Brass.

"Keep walking with your mouth closed, pussy. How's DeAndrea doing?"

Wink looked to be on the verge of words, but instead the hint of tears from his silent laughter took its place. Reece stood there a few seconds longer and then seated himself. "See, niggas like him don't got class baby. You're supposed to wait for them to seat you."

Cydney couldn't care less about what Brass was saying. There was the boss man, the last mark. She tried to ignore it, but she couldn't help but notice how handsome he was. He was the right height and width and the peppermint lingering on his breath had caused her lips to quiver with wanting a taste.

"Wasn't that Reece?"
Wink answered in his usual fashion, on mute, by nodding his head.

"That's the Origami guy from the club," Kyoko said looking over Brass's shoulder for a better look. She was slowly piecing things together.

"Origami guy? Why do you call him that?" Cydney asked Kyoko with an intrigued expression. Brass wasn't feeling the conversation they were having through him like he was invisible.

"Nothing. I'll tell you later."

"Do you think we should invite him to eat with us?" Cydney tried to ask the question without enthusiasm, but it didn't come out that way.

"You're feeling him, ain't you? If you want to take your ass over there and eat with him, go ahead." Brass pushed her by the small of her back towards Reece. She stumbled in her heels.

"I only asked because he's your friend and they consider this lunch time, we seat ourselves," she said pointing to the sign that it was written on.

Late lunch or early dinner, whatever they wanted to call it; it was eaten quietly. Once Brass saw how much he was going to spend on both of their meals, he wanted to hurry up and eat so he could get home to his repayment.

"So what are we doing now?" Kyoko asked hoping someone said a club. She had made a goal to hit a club in every state before she buckled down into a career. It was her first year of college; she only had three years left to accomplish her goal.

"We head back to the house to watch a move and chill. But we're going to hit the liquor store up first," Brass said smashing down the road once he exited the parking lot.

"That's too romantic don't you think? Maybe you should invite Reece."

The car slowed down to a stop and Brass unbuckled his seat belt.

"Aye Wink, grab these hos bags. Never mind, we keeping they shit. Get the fuck out my car. You got about a mile walk back to Reece."

Brass opened the back door and pulled Kyoko out. Cydney got out on her own knowing she'd be thrown out next.

"Can we get our bags, please?"

"Fuck you and those bags. They're mine now." He jumped in the passenger's seat and Wink drove off with Brass hanging out the window yelling, "Welcome to Rock City, dumb stripper bitches."

Cydney pulled out her cell phone, called Chu-Chu, and gave him all the information she gathered.

When she was done, she kicked her heels off and pulled out her sandals from her purse.

"Those fake ballas are gon' to be mad when they see those bags are full of towels."

Cydney turned to tell Kyoko exactly how stupid she found her to be, but the hickey Kyoko had on her neck from Wink made her decide against wasting the time.

*****

Cydney and Kyoko took a cab back to their hotel and stormed in. Cydney was irritated about how things played out, and knew that she should've kept her cards closer to her chest, but time was a luxury that they didn't have. She flopped on one of the beds and pulled out her cellphone. Kyoko walked across the room slowly as she tried to get a feel for Cydney's mood. She knew that she had to be embarrassed. The whole time that she had known her, she had played the role of a diva. To get tossed out on the side of the road like a McDonald's cup had to be demoralizing…for her.

"So…what's the plan now?" Kyoko asked. Cydney held her finger up and spoke into the phone.

"Chu-Chu? Yeah, I got him. I got all of them. They don't even know what's about to happen. Yeah…ok, let me know when y'all make it to town.

Aye, after this is over, we are clear right? Hello?" Cydney looked at the phone and shook her head. She flopped backwards and stared at the ceiling with a heavy sigh. She was about to close her eyes until Kyoko stepped into her field of vision with her arms crossed and gum popping. "What, child?"

"We didn't come here for a good time, huh?" Kyoko asked.

"No, we didn't..." Cydney admitted.

"You're mixed in with the Mexican Mafia. That's tough shit, girl."

"I know, Kyoko. I don't need you to reiterate," Cydney said in an annoyed tone as she closed her eyes.

"What happens to me if you don't hold up your side of the deal?"

"Girl, just relax. Now we wait..."

"Wait for what?" Kyoko sat on the bed beside her.

"We wait and see how things unfold...with Mr. Origami. I see the love marks on your neck, you got the numbers."

*****

Sharpsburg was a large trailer park on the outskirts of Rock City. It mostly housed Mexicans and a small mixture of other races that congregated in the tin slums. A group of Mexicans ran the drug trade in that community, which was mostly meth. They were extremely unorganized, reckless, and only survived so long because they went unchallenged in a small isolated world that the rest of the city forgot about. At the center of the trailer park sat the headquarters of the shaky operation. Five Mexicans sat scattered about the front porch, with blue flags assorted into their attire.

A convoy of six identical Suburbans pulled up in a neat line and parked in front of the trailer. The guys on the porch stood up to observe the sight that looked like the president had just arrived. They watched, waiting in suspense for something to happen and the stillness in the air was a bit eerie. Finally, one of the doors opened and out stepped a large Mexican surrounded by what looked like an army of henchmen.

Chu-Chu sported a fresh tank top over his muscular heavily tattooed body and a pair of dark shades. The first thing he noticed was how chilly NC was compared to the humid air of Arizona. The second thing he noticed was,

"Damn! My soldiers would've already been at the curb with guns drawn by now," he said as he removed his shades and perched them on the top of his head. He looked at the confused Mexicans on the porch and got a fair assessment of what he was dealing with. "Is this how you North Carolinians treat guests of Mexican blood?" One of the figures hopped off the porch and walked across the yard with an exaggerated bop to his step as he held his crotch. Chu-Chu noticed the blue flag that hung from his waist.

"Whatchu need, holmes?" the small figure in front of Chu-Chu asked.

"What set you claim?" Chu-Chu asked curiously.

"Latin Crips!" the guy said animated as he made some sign with his hands.

"Latin Cri...Latin Crips? The fuck?" He turned to Tonto. "Aye, pull out that smart little gizmo of yours and please tell me what the fuck a Latin Crip is." Tonto pulled out his cellphone and went to typing. Chu-Chu looked at the guy in front of him. "Did you mean Latin Kings?" he asked, giving the man a chance to save face.

"Nah, Holmes...Latin Crips!" He made the sign again. His crew hopped off the porch and joined him now, from a safe distance.

Tonto looked up at Chu-Chu from his phone and shrugged. "See, even Mr. Google has never heard of a Latin Crip. The fuck kind of operation you chulos got going on here?" The crew remained silent. "Matter of fact, fuck this shit, who is in charge?" he asked defiantly. The man in front of him took a step forward.

"Me...why?"

Chu-Chu smiled, reached behind his back, pulled out a pistol, and shot the man square in the face. The bullet exited the back of his head and struck the porch, barely missing a frightened member of his crew. Before the body hit the ground, his crew pulled out pistols, but Chu-Chu's men had them out numbered, and out gunned.

"I'll ask again," Chu-Chu said as he wiped the speckled blood from his face with the back of his hand. "Who is in charge?" The remaining four all dropped their weapons and raised their arms in surrender. "Good answer," Chu-Chu said as his men collected the discarded weapons. He walked past them and sat at the edge of the porch with his Nike Cortez's swinging like an entertained child. He winked at Tonto who pulled out two knives and tossed them in the center of the yielding crew. "While I'm in town, I feel that it is my duty to fix the Latin image that you chulos have so blatantly disrespected. The thing is," he pointed as his ensemble of henchmen. "We don't really have room for old blood. Maybe only like…two spots, ya know?" The crew looked down at the knives and back at Chu-Chu. "You two, versus you two. The winning team joins the winning team."

The four men hesitated as eyes bounced from the weapons to the other faces who were probably having the same thoughts. Finally, the two guys on the right grabbed the knives and held them outward to kill the opposing squad. Right when they were about to strike, two shots erupted from Tonto's pistols, colliding with the skulls of the men with the knives. The two remaining members watched as their old friends fell lifelessly into the yard, creating pools of blood and brain matter to fertilize the lawn. They nervously turned their focus to Chu-Chu, who was obviously calling the shots.

"Any chulo willing to kill his brother, just to survive, is no brother of mines. We don't fold under pressure, you two understand?" They nodded, probably because he pointed at them with the pistol. "Good!" He hopped off the porch and clasped his hands together as he looked around his new environment. "Now, where do you hide bodies around here? Where is the nearest desert?" They looked at him dumbfounded. "What?"

*****

Rock City was a small town, so word got around quicker than a poodle in heat. Reece was nervous as he stood at the door of Unc's office with his hand on the knob. He was extremely hesitant to enter, not knowing what was waiting for him on the other side. Unc sounded irate on the phone when he summoned him, and ended the call quickly. The only theory Reece had at the moment was the fact maybe Brass went ahead and spilled the beans once he was discovered at the restaurant. Brass knew that Reece had something on him when he saw him with the witness of the murders, but Reece also knew that Unc wouldn't give a shit about that if Brass alarmed him of the affair first.

Reece sighed and turned the knob. Wink was standing off to the side while Brass sat in front of a tight faced Unc. Reece strolled over to his seat and easily sat down as he glanced at Brass trying to keep an eye on him. His other mission was to keep Wink in his peripheral…just in case.

"I swear I dunno why I trusted you…" Unc started as he rubbed his face in frustration. Reece could feel his heartbeat increase in torque. He glanced over at Brass again, but he looked just as confused as Reece did. Brass adjusted himself in his seat. He prayed that Unc didn't find out about Reece and his wife on his own. Maybe DeAndrea went ahead and told him in attempt to save her own ass. If that were true, then Brass wouldn't have a card to play on. He couldn't admit that he already knew, out of fear of being punished for not informing the boss. "All I asked you fuckers to do was what the fuck I paid you for!" Unc slammed his fist on the desk. Recce and Brass looked at each other.

"Wh…What's going on, Unc?" Reece asked. Unc slowly raised his head and scowled at him.

"What's going on? I'll tell you exactly what's fucking going on. Didn't I tell you to be fucking careful in Arizona? Didn't I tell you dumb fucks to get in and get out unseen?" Reece and Brass nodded. "Then where was the miscommunication?" Unc spread his large arms within his white silk button-up. The tail of the shirt was untucked under his girth.

"I'm not tracking…what happened?"

"That fucking Mexican that you killed in the club to get to D-Rock. Who was he?" Unc asked as he calmed his voice and crossed his arms. He walked around the desk and sat at the edge of it, letting his eyes bounce from Brass to Reece, forcing himself to patiently wait on an answer.

"I mean…he was just some Mexican. Shit, he was about to kill D-Rock his damn self," Brass threw in, foolishly thinking that he was helping the situation.

"Then you should've let him!" Unc said as he stood to his feet and pointed at Brass in rage. "I'll tell you who he was. He was part of the Mexican Mafia, my sources say." Reece gave him a perplexed look. "Oh yeah, fucker. I have sources…reliable sources. I wish I could say the same about you." He flopped down in the executive chair and interlocked his fingers across his chest, trying his best to calm down and not have a heart attack.

"So…what's the problem?" Brass asked.

Unc had to pinch his eyes close before he jumped out of his skin.

"The problem is, now I hear there is a damn army of Mexican Mafia muhterfuckers in Rock City!" Unc leaned across the desk. "And guess who they are asking for?" Reece looked at Brass and frowned his face up. Brass had really fucked up this time. Now his hormones were going to cost them their lives or at least their freedom. How did he find that stripper, and why was she in town? It was all coming together…she was in on it. "Wink, Brass," Unc started as he pointed at them individually. "And somebody named Bossman, which I assume is supposed to be yo' ass!" Unc said as his finger landed on Reece.

"Unc, I dunno how this could've-" Reece started but Unc shot to his feet, snatched the lamp from his desk, and slung it across the room, shattering the porcelain against the wall beside Wink.

"Shut the fuck up! You niggas have become nothing but liabilities!" He eased back into his chair and shook his head. "There's no telling how this will end…a fucking shit storm!"

"So what do we do now?" Reece asked, hoping for a chance to fall back into the boss man's good graces.

"We? Nah, y'all can get the fuck out of my office. I'll figure this out my damn self." Reece and Brass stayed seated, both not wanting to leave on that note. "I'm serious, GET THE FUCK OUT!" Unc roared. Reece followed Brass and Wink to their car and let Brass get in. Just as he started the vehicle, Reece leaned in with a glare.

"I guess we are even now, nigga," Reece said.

"The fuck you mean, even?" Brass jerked his head back in shock. "Nigga, you sleeping with the nigga wife!"

"And you invited some bitch to town who brought the fucking Mexican Mafia with her! You basically snitched!" Reece spat.

"Don't call me no fucking snitch, you snake! Sleeping with your man's wife and shit. How are your hormones justified and mines not?"

"'Cause my dick didn't lead us into a fucking war! Which sin do you think is greater in Unc's eyes? And before you answer, I need you to think about what D-Rock got," Reece said as he stepped away slowly. "This fuck up is on you, Brass…both of you niggas…"

*****

Reece's mind was everywhere but the present. He parked his car in his driveway and stepped out into the night air. The moon was full and enormous, seeming to almost swallow the earth, or maybe that was just in his mind as he felt as if the sky was falling. The Mexicans were in town declaring war. Unc had lost all faith in him. DeAndrea was on his nerves making him regret ever entering the walls of her pussy or her heart, and not to mention, Brass knew his secret and was practically blackmailing him into bowing out. None of that would matter if the Mexican Mafia caught up to them first.

As Reece dangled his keys in his hand and walked up his steps, something small on his doormat caught his eye. He stepped forward cautiously, thinking that it was a bug of some sort, and he didn't fuck with bugs, at all, but it wasn't. He looked around and squatted down to the item. Feeling his heart beat increase in RPMs he picked the object up and held it in his palm as he tried to make sense of it. He stared with his mouth ajar at the $100 bill folded into an origami crane. Before his mind could register facts, he felt the barrel of a pistol rest at the back of his head.

"Money is such a distraction; don't you think?" a soft voice asked from behind him. At first, he thought it was the Asian stripper since she was the only one on earth who knew part of his secret, but as he stood up and looked through the reflection of his glass door, he saw the other woman...the one that he chose to let live. "Let's go inside, Bossman."

Trying to tame his fingers from shaking, he inserted his key in the door and pushed it open. She followed him in and locked the door behind her.

"What do you want? If this is about that Mexican dude, then I must apologize. He was just collateral damage," Reece said as he stepped in the living room and tossed his keys onto the coffee table. He was trying to stay calm and see where her head was.

"Shut that shit up! I'm not here about him."
Reece turned and faced her. He observed her body as his eyes traced the curves of her black dress like a canyon trail. She was beautiful...too beautiful to be pointing a gun towards him and working for the Mexican Mafia. She looked more like a businesswoman- the type you'd see walking hurriedly down the sidewalks of Times Square. She didn't seem like a killer, but Reece couldn't bet his life on that theory...not that theory.

"So the Grim Reaper does wear black?" Reece asked with a pinch of charm as he folded his arms.

"Flattering, but it won't work on me. I hear compliments all day, honey," she said as she licked her lips. "Queens aren't moved by the praises of peasants."

"Is that what you think I am? A peasant? You just called me Bossman. Your theories contradict each other," Reece said as he stepped forward. Cydney pulled the hammer back on the revolver to remind him of the threat.

"Enough of the bullshit. You and your goons killed my worker and in turn flipped my whole business upside down. Now I need retribution."

"Business? So you're not a stripper?" Reece asked as he raised a brow.

"If you ever believed that, then you are as stupid as your counterpart. Stop stalling and show me the safe!" she said as she pointed down the hall. All she came for was the money so she could skip town and head back to New York. She planned on setting up shop there, but she'd need money to lay a solid foundation. Of course, she had a nice chunk of change stashed away in Arizona, but she was sure that Chu-Chu had men watching her spots. That money was tied up, and it was too risky for her to return until her business arrangement with him was settled. The thing was, she didn't have time to wait for the Mexican Mafia to kill who they came for. She needed to get away ASAP.

"The safe?" Reece shrugged. "I don't have one...I hate to tell you this, but you have the wrong guy. I'm not the boss of this operation. I'm merely an advisor."

Cydney blinked hard, letting his words sink again, and then shook her head aggressively.

"Shut that shit up! Go!" she said as she pointed down the hall to his bedroom. He led her inside as she surveyed the room for signs of a stash. "The closet...open it."

"Listen, you don't have to do this, ok? Just leave now and I'll act like this scene never happened," Reece warned.

"Boy, you must think I came all this way to play games or some shit! Open the fucking closet!"

"I can't do that," Reece said as he lowered his hands. He was taking a risk, but he really didn't want her to see what was inside.

"Ok," Cydney said as she marched over and snatched the door open while keeping her gun pointed at Reece. She flicked on the light inside and paused in her tracks. "What's this?"

"It's nothing," Reece said as he sat at the edge of the bed and rubbed his palms over his face.

Cydney looked closer at the large glass trophy case and inside she saw what seemed to be hundreds of neatly placed origami cranes folded out of $100 bills. Intrigued, she stepped out of the closet and looked at him. She could see the shame written all over his face, which only spiked her curiosity.

"Why do you do this? What do they mean? What is it with you and these paper ducks?" Cydney asked as she unintentionally lowered her weapon.

"They're cranes...and it's nothing...just some stupid theory...an old Japanese legend," Reece said as he turned his head and stared at the corner. In it was the duffle bag of money that he was supposed to be coming up with a venture to invest in for Unc. That deal was probably off the table now, even though Reece doubted he'd live to confirm.

"The Origami Theory? Making something out of paper..." Cydney said. Reece looked at her in shock.

"Something like that. It's not much of a stash, but you can take it. Go ahead," Reece offered, hoping to distract her from the duffle bag.

"My grandfather taught me that," Cydney said as she sat on the bed beside him. Reece was shocked at how comfortable she had become. All he had to do was reach over, punch her, and take the weapon...but she didn't seem to care. "He always said, take your money and fold it, invest time into it, and make something beautiful out of it," she said as she rubbed her temples with the pistol still in her hand. "I never knew what that shit meant, but I dedicated my life to it. Maybe you can tell me?" she said as she turned towards Reece. She was now aiming a different weapon at him, more deadly than the first, and they were akimbo. She pointed her eyes at his, neutralizing him with her stare.

"I dunno what your grandfather meant; all I know is the legend. If you fold a thousand cranes you'll be granted fortune, and eternal peace…also a wish." Reece was hesitant to mention the wish part, knowing how childish it might seemed.

"And what's your wish?" Cydney asked, sounding more like a date trying to get to know him than an executioner.

"To leave this life. Start a business…invest this ugly money into something-" he locked eyes with her Medusa stare. "Something beautiful…"

Cydney smiled but caught herself, so she jumped up to her feet.

"1,000 cranes huh? How many do you have?" she asked as she peeked back into the closet.

"427…" he said. "Three of them came from Arizona…" She looked at him with a puzzled expression.

"What do you mean? Why not just go ahead and fold 1,000 of them. I'm sure you have the bills in that duffle bag over there."

"It's not that simple," he said as he stood to his feet. "I only make one when someone dies that I'm somehow responsible for." She raised a brow and looked back at the trophy case.

"So you're telling me that you've killed 427 people?"

"I'm telling you that 427 people have died under my regime."

"I thought you were just an advisor?" Cydney questioned. She took a step back but Reece kept stepping towards her.

"I am, I work for the true boss man, but whenever there is a death, whether it be a murder, or a drug overdose, or even an abortion or a soldier getting life in the bing...I make a crane..."

Before Cydney realized it, he had his hands on her shoulders, returning her traumatic stare. She pulled herself together and stepped away from him.

"Your boss is going to die...you know that right?" she asked as she walked away, refusing to face him.

"I know...I tried to steer him out of this life and get him to invest in a legit business. That's what that money over there is for, but he's too far gone in the streets. He won't listen."

"Invest in me," Cydney said as she turned and faced him.

"What?" Reece let out a chuckle. "You have the gun. Take the money, killer."

"That's not how I want it. I need a new business partner. Especially since you killed my old one."

"Why would I do that? You can't have much going for yourself if you're here to rob me."

"I'm a businesswoman. I always have shit going for me. I have a staffing agency within a general labor-staffing agency. My workers paint, drive forklifts, act as secretaries, work on highways, hell, they do whatever it takes to make money and I get 30% of it."

"How? What do you get 30% for?"

"For granting them their freedom. I work at the immigration office and I get people coming in and out from all over the world. Some want to call America their home and some come only to work on a project or for school. America doesn't just grant people permission to come over here, there's a process and if they want that process sped up; they pay me. I provide jobs for those that don't have one to ensure they pay me."

"And what if they don't pay?" Reece was interested but he needed to hear all the details. There was no way he'd invest without knowing all the ins and outs of her scheme.

"Well, you just killed my muscle and business partner. The Mexican guy owned the staffing agency that I sent my people to and for each head I sent him, I earned 5%. Now you understand why I was robbing you, you've cost me money," she said before continuing. "Anyways, Tomas also acted as the devil for me. If I didn't receive my pay he had a way to get it."

"So you're asking me to be your killer? So what do you need my money for?"

Cydney hadn't fully thought out a plan for his investment. Hell, she never thought they would be having this conversation but she knew what she needed.

"No, if they don't pay me I can deport their assess. What I need you to do is invest in a staffing agency. I would still need my 5% for sending you clients and I would continue to take my 30% off the backend."

"You get 35% and I'm stuck paying the overhead of running a company? How does that sound like a smart investment for me?" One and one wasn't adding up to two and she was losing his interest.

"The strip club you open will bring the revenue to cover both businesses. There's 22 strippers at five different strip clubs that pay me $200.00 every day they perform. Changing location will mean I'd have to start over with set up but the ones I have currently working for me will continue. You will charge my workers 30% of what they make each night and the other strippers 20%. Then you can collect my money from the strippers and keep 50% of it and send me the other half."

"I think you need to go back to the drawing board. You're telling me that you want me to agree to you making an 85% profit off both schemes and I make 80% at the most? I though a partnership is 50/50? I'm short 5%." He liked the plan but wasn't feeling the numbers.

"How don't you see that you're winning? You make contracts with the company you send clients to and get paid for them. You're also charging people to get into the club and for overpriced drinks. Your businesses will cover the overhead and everything you get from working with me is profit."

Reece leaned against the dresser and folded his arms.

"If this has been working for you, you should have enough money to invest in all this yourself. Seems to me like you don't need my money. You have it all figured out."

"I don't need the money, I want it...I want you..." she said as she stepped in his face. She leaned so close that their lips almost touched. She could smell his cologne mixing with her perfume in harmony.

"Is that right?"

"The Mexican Mafia is going to kill your boss and Brass' dumbass. You don't have much time to convince your boss to invest in this opportunity... a few days, tops."

"How do we know that you are legit and you're not trying to fuck us?"

Cydney leaned in and kissed his lips softly, sucking on his bottom lip as she pulled away. "You don't." She pulled out her cellphone and texted Kyoko who was parked down the street in the rental to come pick her up. "But if your boss dies and that money gets taken by the state, or his wife, or somebody, then you just missed out. Unless no one knows you have it and you keep it," Cydney said with a smile. "You have a few days…"

Reece followed her out the door and held the screen as she looked back with a smile before entering the rental. He smiled back and locked eyes with Kyoko in the driver's seat. He didn't know if he could trust the woman, but he did know that he was running out of options, and all of the walls seemed to be closing in on him.

He closed the door and went back inside, oblivious to the other car that was parked down the street watching the woman exit his house. DeAndrea sat up in her seat when he went in the house as rage boiled to her face. She felt like steam was about to sprout from her eyes like a cartoon. That was why he had been so distant to her lately. He had another chick threatening to take her place.

With Brass knowing their secret, and now Reece betraying her in deceit, DeAndrea knew that she had to look out for herself. A storm was coming and she assured herself that she wasn't going to be the only one who got wet...

The Flipside

The ride back to the hotel was spent with both ladies stuck in their thoughts. Cydney was trying to come up with a business proposal to present to Reece, and Kyoko was wondering when she would be paid. The silence was broken when Kyoko slammed their hotel room's door.

"Why did you slam the door?" Cydney put her purse on the table and kicked off her shoes.

"Where's the money? You said we were going to rob Bossman. I thought that was the plan?"

Kyoko was pissed. She had gone the extra mile to get Reece's cellphone number like Cydney had asked of her. However, she never imagined the mile would lead to her knees and a mouthful of Wink next to a piss-filled urinal in the men's restroom at the restaurant. It wasn't a secret that she provided lip service from time to time in the VIP rooms of the strip club, but she was paid for it. Heavy silence in the car on the ride to the hotel made her think Cydney was playing her for a fool.

"You promised if I got the information you would break me off. I sucked it out of him and all I got was this nasty looking hickey, where is my money?"

"I got the money." Cydney said rolling her eyes. "But I invested it. Don't worry, you'll get paid soon."

"No." Kyoko stomped her feet like an unruly child. "I get paid for my services, now. You said get the cellphone number. If it weren't for me tracking him down by his phone's GPS, you wouldn't have known where he was. Now I'm involved in this bullshit because I followed your rules. If you want me to continue to, show me some green."

Cydney could tell by the glint in her eyes that Kyoko meant business. She had a couple of hundreds in her purse she was going to use to pacify the whining baby in front of her but Kyoko had fucked it up.

"You blackmail me and everybody that has to deal with you in Arizona. If you want me to be your homegirl, pay me or I'll blackmail you."

"And how do you plan on doing that?"

Kyoko was feeling her newfound authority too much for Cydney's liking.

"I'll tell. I'll tell on what you've been doing to us at the immigration department. I'll tell them what you force us to do to live in America." She snatched the gun out of Cydney's open purse. "Bitch, I'm not scared of you and without Tomas, no one is. If you don't want to get shot and we become real home girls than pay me. Pay me now."

Cydney couldn't help but to smile. Kyoko had heart and she admired her for it, but she had flexed on the wrong person.

"You dumb little strip ho. Do you really think waving a gun in my face scares me? The Mexican Mafia wants to kill me and we're in North Carolina with tree climbing country boys that want me dead too. In addition, I'm supposed to be scared of you? Bitch, please."

She charged at Kyoko and went to snatch the gun out of her hand. To her surprise, Kyoko never pulled the trigger. Even if she would have, it was a B.B gun she bought at Walmart that morning. The pellet would have hurt, but it wouldn't have killed her. Once the gun had switched hands, Cydney took the safety off, cocked it to pump the air into it, and then shot her in the calf muscle with it.

"Did your dumb ass see me check-in a gun at the airport? That's what I went to Walmart for."

Her words were drowned out by Kyoko's screams of bloody murder. She thought a real gun had shot her. She fell to floor between the double beds holding her knee of her wounded leg. There wasn't a drop of blood anywhere. Her thick white slouch socks didn't allow the steel plated in copper

B.B to penetrate her flesh, but Kyoko didn't know it.

"Call the ambulance please before I bleed to death. I have thin blood... I don't want to die in America."

"Bitch look." She grabbed Kyoko by her bone straight ponytail and forced her to look at her calf. "No blood, now shut your loud ass up and get off the floor."

"I'm not dying?" Kyoko sniffled.

"No ho, not yet anyways."

"Housekeeping, is everything okay in there? We have reports of yelling and screaming coming from your room." The question had been asked but the knocking on the door didn't stop.

"Yes, my friend hit her pinky toe on the base of the dresser. She's fine, thanks."

The knocks continued.

"I'm sorry ma'am but it's hotel policy for us to do a visual check. Can you please open the door or we will have to call the police to escort us in."
Cydney helped Kyoko to her feet and then dragged her to the door. She opened just enough to reveal their faces.

"You see, she's fine. A little clumsy at times, but fine. Thanks for checking."

She tried to close the door but the housekeeper placed her stiletto in it.

"We value you as our guest but I need to do a walk through inspection to ensure there was no damage done to our property."

She was the sexiest dressed housekeeper both women had ever seen. The solid blue form fitting dressed revealed all of her bountiful legs, thighs, hips, and breasts. Her makeup was perfect and every curl on her head was flawless. It wasn't until the woman pushed her cleaning cart to the center of the room that Cydney thought about checking her credentials.

"So… you're from housekeeping?" Cydney's index finger pointed at her heels and then up to her wand curls. "Where's your name tag? All the other ones wore one but they weren't dressed like you."

"I'm sorry, I came straight from my sister's engagement party so I didn't have time to change but I have my badge, it's right here." DeAndrea lifted the stack of towels and retrieved the gun and Taser she had concealed. "Now sit your asses on the bed."

Walking backwards, she made her way to the door and locked it. Next, she turned the volume up on the television and then returned to her hostages.

"Who is this crazy bitch?" Kyoko tried to whisper it but the sound of the Taser being cut on informed her how loud she really was.

"I'm the crazy bitch that's going to tase you in your pretty little egg roll face until it burns and bubbles up like a whitehead. I don't play with hos about my man."

"Wait, your man said he was single. The queen of IG don't fuck with men who got baby mama, side chicks, wife, jerri curls, E.D., bi-sexual..."

"Shut the fuck up," Cydney and DeAndrea yelled in unison.

"Don't play stupid with me, bitch. I know your friend is fucking my man Reece."

"You know Reece too? Everybody knows Reece," Kyoko said with her eyes locked on the BB gun less than a foot away from her on the nightstand. "You're Reece's bitch?"

Cydney elbowed Kyoko in her side and was met by volts of electricity surging through her body via her back. It was now Cydney's screams filling the room while Kyoko watched in horror.

"How long have you been fucking my man, fat bitch?"

Cydney wanted to answer but the electricity took ownership of her voice. She had been shock by static electricity but she never experienced electricity flowing and burning through her body like that. She reached out to Kyoko for help but she moved away. She didn't want the electricity to flow through her from Cydney's touch. The quick movement of Kyoko caused DeAndrea to turn off the Taser and point her gun at her.

"Spill it bitch, I want to know everything about you and Reece."

"There's nothing to tell, he's not my man, nor are we being sexual." Cydney slowly regained her composure but the Taser was turned back on and placed a breath away from her lips.

"I'll ask you one more time or maybe I won't." When Cydney saw the blue and yellow strip of electricity spread across the mouth of the Taser she spoke up.

"Arizona. I met him, Brass, and Wink in Arizona."

DeAndrea knew of the trip to dispose of D-Rock but knew nothing of there being women involved.

"You met him in Arizona, and?" She moved the Taser from Cydney's mouth to the bottom of her dangling gold earring and let the spark meet the metal. The earring acted as a conductor and in seconds, the portion pierced through her earlobe burned her skin. She snatched the earring out with a scream.

"They killed some guys at the strip club she works at," she said pointing a finger at Kyoko. "And now the victim's family thinks we had something to do with so we came here to ask for their help."

"Is that the truth?" DeAndrea asked pointing the gun at Kyoko and she shook her head no.

"They think she had something to do with it, not me. She came here for help, I came to party and I'm loving those stilettos, mommy. We should go to a club."

DeAndre wasn't going to try and fathom how Kyoko could be so dumb. What she really wanted now was details. She kept her hands on both weapons but joined the women on the bed.

"What's your names?"

"I'm Kyoko but the world knows me as the Queen of the Selfie and that's God. She likes to make people call her that. Her real name is Cydney though. Do you have any gum? God threw my new pack away."

Silently, Cydney prayed DeAndrea would put her out of her misery by putting a bullet through Kyoko's head but it was her words DeAndrea wanted to hear.

"God? Why did you say that?"

Kyoko poured the tea and then brewed some more as she broke down Cydney's immigration scheme. She poured the last drop when she said, "And your man killed Tomas so she can't be God anymore."

"Oh, so this is a revenge mission." Jumping to her feet, she pointed her gun to the side of Cydney's head.

"No, this is a cleanup mission," Cydney countered.

She picked up the story where Kyoko left off telling about Tomas' ties to the Mexican Mafia and them putting a hit over her head if she didn't help find the people who killed him.

"I came to North Carolina to see if your man and his friends could help us with that."

"I think we can help each other..," DeAndrea said as she started pacing. Cydney cut her eyes at Kyoko and then at DeAndrea.

"What do you have in mind?"

"Your people-"

"They're not my people," Cydney corrected her.

"Whoever the fuck they are! They want the people responsible for whatever happened in Arizona." DeAndrea stopped in her tracks and smiled at Cydney. "So, we will give them to them. We will give them the real boss, my husband."

"Why would you give up your husband...oh," Cydney dropped her head and smiled as the lightbulb in her head finally flicked on. The woman standing in front of her was just as cold to the touch as she was. "You want your husband dead so you can be with Reece unconditioned. I get it..."

"We both need Reece alive, for different reasons I hope." DeAndrea held a stare with her for her point to sink in. "This way everyone wins. We give them my husband, and the other cronies that I don't give two shits about, and we all..." She sat down on the mattress beside Cydney and leaned into her face. "We all live happily ever after." She looked over at Cydney's purse, reached inside and pulled out one of her business cards that had her cellphone number on it. She got to her feet and read the card over as she walked blindly to the door. "I'll be in touch with the details. Just make sure that your people are on stand-by," she said as she exited.

Cydney stood to her feet and looked at Kyoko who was busy surfing the web on her phone as if nothing had just happened. She envied the child's mind. Ignorance was truly bliss. Cydney grabbed her cellphone and called Chu-Chu.

"Aye, I got what you need..."

"Is that so, boss lady? I was beginning to lose faith in you," Chu-Chu said as Latin rap music blared in the background. He was settling nicely in the new town.

"Yeah, dig this. The boss that ordered the hit, his wife wants him to take a vacation. She's willing to deliver him to a said location, but she wants this 'getaway' to be a surprise, you feel me?" Cydney was impressed with how fast she came up with the decoded analogy. Kyoko looked at her and rolled her eyes. "What do you say? We even?"

"I may know a travel agent who can arrange the trip," Chu-Chu said before clearing his throat. He walked to a quieter surrounding and shut the door behind him. "The wife..." he started. "Is she taking an unexpected trip as well?"

Cydney smiled into the phone. "Board that bitch too." She hung up and felt the stare from Kyoko.

"What?"

"You are one cold bitch, you know that?"

"It's a cold world, baby girl. You can adapt and weather it, or you can fold..."

"You're smart boss lady! But," Kyoko said putting her headphones over her ears and then she spoke in Japanese, "ketsueki okane ga bai wa..."

Cydney laughed, "What does all that mean?"

She heard her question but pretended not to. Kyoko had laced her meaningless compliment with the warning that blood money don't fold.

Paper Cuts

"I'm saying though," Brass stated as he navigated the Wrangler down the dark avenue. He and Wink were cruising the streets with the doors and the top off of the vehicle, feeling like field generals assessing the potential casualties of war. "This shit gon' get messy. Them Mexican Mafia niggas didn't come all of this way for nothing. They are looking for blood, and to potentially set-up shop. Watch what I tell you now," Brass said as he offered Wink the blunt. He refused and kept his eyes focused on their surroundings while Brass rambled. "Then this trifling ass nigga Reece got Unc distracted and shit. Talking all that legit shit. Fuck all that! We need to be focusing on home…focusing on what made us!"

He stopped at the light and took a deep pull of the blunt. Just as Wink looked to his right, a lowered Crown Vic pulled up alongside them. As the tinted window rolled down, Wink reached for his weapon on his hip but he was too late. Tonto appeared holding a sawed off shotgun.

"Que Pasa?" he said as he squeezed the trigger. The buckshot spread hit Wink in his chest, tossing his body nearly into the driver's seat.

Brass realized what was going on and stomped on the gas. The Wrangler's large mud tires peeled in the streets as the Jeep launched forward. With one arm on the wheel, Brass pushed Wink over and tried to sit him up straight.

"Wink! Yo, nigga! You good?" Brass asked as he kept his eyes on the road and the speeding vehicle that was rapidly approaching from the rear. He looked over and saw the carnage that had been made of Wink's chest, and felt his heart drop. His man was gone. As he stared at his partner, he felt the surface of the road changed and looked up just time to notice that he had drifted off into the field.

Tonto and his crew followed the Jeep into the field as he hung out the window firing shots, trying to get lucky.

"Catch them fools!" Tonto screamed from the backseat to his driver. His body jerked in the window frame as the car navigated across the rough terrain through clouds of dust but Tonto kept firing. Brass knew that he had the upper hand off-road, so he reached over and grabbed Wink's gun from the floor. Without looking, he aimed backwards and fired wild shots at his pursuers. He wanted to pull over and shoot it out, but he had to play it smart. He only had one gun, and there was no telling how many Mexicans were chasing him. He needed to get away. He fired his last shot as the slide of the weapon locked back, and tossed it out of the vehicle. Gripping the wheel with rage, he took the Jeep down a narrow path in the woods, as tree branches slapped him in the face like nature's gauntlet- rather that than a bullet in the face.

He glanced up at the mirror and saw the headlights of the Crown Vic still behind him. He made a wild turn as the Jeep spun around 180 degrees, making a screen of dust. The Crown Vic sped up through the cloud just as he exited it going the opposite way. Tonto fired a wild shot at him and the cunning move till he looked forward just in time for their car to collide with a tree; flinging him from the window like a mechanical bull.

Brass looked back and saw the taillights stalled against the tree as the cloud dispersed. He had made it out alive, but he couldn't say the same for his counterpart. Once he got down the road, he stopped and pulled his friend out of the Jeep. He laid his body down on the side of the road, where it was sure to be found shortly by a commuter. He kneeled beside his friend as Wink's eyes stared at him lifelessly. Brass let a single teardrop fall as he closed Wink's eyelids with his fingers.

"These niggas gon' pay for this, bro…"

******

"Is Reece driving us?" Unc asked as he stepped out of the door and approached his wife. She locked arms with him as he glanced over her tight black dress. They both looked casket ready as they headed to the awaiting limo. It was their anniversary, and against his better judgment, Unc let her talk him into going out for a nice dinner to celebrate.

"No, he isn't. Why does that matter?" DeAndrea asked as she clutched her purse and let him open the door for her.

"I'd just feel safer with him behind the wheel, ya know?" Unc said as he slid in beside her and closed the door. DeAndrea tapped on the tinted window that divided them and let the driver know to pull off.

"Tonight is our night. I don't want any of your little associates around to distract you from enjoying yourself. You understand?" DeAndrea said as she smiled at him. Not giving him a chance to reply she rubbed her palm across his lap, and as if she had a magnet on her hand, his dick shot upwards. She unzipped his slacks and started massaging his shaft with her soft hands as she leaned forward with kisses on his neck. "How about a little dessert before dinner?" she asked.

"What's on the menu?" Unc played along.

"Hopefully cream pie." She smiled and brought her full lips to his throbbing dick. The warmness of her mouth made him lean back in ecstasy as he placed his hand gently behind her head. She knew exactly how to suck the nut out of him, and bring him to his knees. She sucked as she stroked with one hand while cupping his balls with the other. She felt his sack tighten up, she stopped and pulled her dress up to her waist. He opened his eyes for the first time in minutes and watched as she hovered over his lap, and guided his tip through the entrance of her water slide.

"Shit..." Unc said as he leaned his head back. She gyrated her hips slowly as she teased the tip of his dick and then slammed down on him. She knew he was on the verge of nutting just from the way his fingers were twisting up like he was throwing gang signs. She sped up her movements as he exploded inside her, filling her canal up with his warm sperm. His mouth was stuck ajar as his body tensed up. When he opened his eyes again, he noticed the limo had stopped. He looked around and then at DeAndrea who was smiling at him.

A black Suburban pulled up beside his window.

"Driver! Pull off!" Unc screamed as he pushed DeAndrea off of him. The divider lowered and Unc saw the tattooed face appear.

"No hablo English," Chu-Chu said with a grin. Unc froze as he gripped his zipper.

"I figured the first wound should come from me," DeAndrea said as she reached into her purse and pulled out a small knife. Before he could react, she shoved it into his side and twisted it. He cringed at the pain as his head hit the window, just as the Suburban's windows lowered and two Hispanic gunmen appeared. DeAndrea kissed him on the cheek and then rolled out of the opposite door just at the shots began. She hit the asphalt and covered her face as glass fell on her like confetti. She hated that she set her husband up, but it was something that needed to be done. As she tried to crawl across the street, the driver ran up to her. "I don't need help, go finish the job!" she barked at him.

"I am…" Chu-Chu said. She looked up at him and screamed as he aimed the gun at her and fired a single shot into her stomach. He tucked his weapon and walked back to the scene. The gunmen ceased fire when their boss walked back up. He opened Unc's riddled door and peeked inside. There was no need to check his pulse. Bullets and glass ripped off his face, and every inch of his body was hit.

"This is for Tomas," Chu-Chu said as he fired an extra shot into Unc's skull for good measure.

He slammed the door as one of his henchmen tapped him on the arm and pointed across the street. He looked and saw DeAndrea limping towards a car that was waving her over.

"Should we go finish that?"

"Nah...let her die slow," Chu-Chu ordered as he and his men climbed in the Suburban and peeled off.

"Lady, hurry up before they start shooting again!" the Good Samaritan coached as he helped her to her feet. He looked over her wound and cringed at the sight of all the blood. "Let's get you to the hospital," he said as he opened the backdoor.

"No hospital..." DeAndrea said in a faint voice as she leaned against the car.

"Ma'am," the guy said as he looked at her with his blue eyes. His thin blonde hair danced on top of his head to the soft chords of the wind. "You're losing a lot of blood. You could die."

"I said no hospital!" she shouted as she pulled out the bloody knife and slashed at him. He jumped back and fell to his ass as he scuffled away in the dirt.

"You're a fucking nut!" he shouted as he ran away and disappeared down the street. DeAndrea slowly climbed into his vehicle and pulled off.

*****

"Have you spoke to your boss yet?" Reece read the text from Cydney. He had been riding around for hours, thinking of an angle to present the proposition to Unc. Cydney's opportunity was just what he needed to push Unc in the right direction, but the war with the Mexicans was becoming a distraction. Then there was the issue with Brass. How long would he remain quiet and bite his tongue on Reece's little secret? The fact that Reece knew that Brass inadvertently invited the Mexican Mafia to their city in his own foolish way; that leverage would only last so long. As soon as the beef was handled, if Brass lived to see the next day, he'd spill the beans on Unc's desk, and lick his fingers as he stirred it up.

"Not yet. Just riding around thinking," Reece replied and placed the phone on the passenger seat. Stopping at a light, he saw ambulance led by two police cars zip by with the sirens blaring. He just shook his head at the scene. There was no telling what happened.

"Maybe you should go see him...you know...to make sure your ducks are in order."

Reece didn't fully understand her response, but he was in the area. He took a deep sigh and decided to ride by Unc's manor. Hopefully, the old man would be sleep, resting his eyes, and Reece would spare his nerves for another day.

Reece pulled up and noticed that the door was wide open, and an unfamiliar car was parked wildly in front of the steps. A trail of blood led into the house, causing Reece to pull out his pistol and creep in. He needed to call Brass, but didn't have time, so he leaned against the porch column for cover and sent Brass a text.

"I'm at Unc's. Some shit went down. Come thru!" was all he had a chance to type before he hit send. He heard something fall, deep inside of the house.

Reece gripped his pistol, followed the trail of blood, and tiptoed up the stairs. It looked like whoever was bleeding made their way to Unc's office. Reece had to swallow hard at the thought that it was Unc. He closed his eyes as he slid against the wall and up the stairs, saying a quick prayer. As he got closer to the door, he could hear footsteps inside the office, followed by grunts. *It has to be Unc! He's hurt!* Reece thought as he bolted in the room. He slammed on his brakes, sliding on his heels when he saw DeAndrea hunched over the safe in the corner, stuffing money in a bag.

"What are you doing, D?" Reece asked. She snapped her head in his direction and stood to her feet. She tossed the bag of money behind the desk and looked at him with pitiful eyes. Reece looked at her stomach and saw the gunshot surrounded by dried blood and fresh plasma that continued to ooze.

"What happened to you?" Reece asked as he stepped forward and placed his gun on the edge of the desk. She fell forward into his arms as he held her up.

"They killed him..." she uttered in a faint voice.

"Who? Unc? He's dead?" Reece asked as he leaned back to look at her face. She nodded as tears fled her sockets. "Who?"

"The Mexicans...I barely made it out alive, Ree-" she broke into a coughing fit, and Reece held her close as the news of his slain boss had failed to register in his head. "They betrayed me..." she said.

Reece just held her and slowly rocked her side to side.

"It's ok, baby. Everything will be alright, you hear me...we just have to get you to a hos..." He paused and looked at her again. "What do you mean they betrayed you?" Reece asked. She refused to look at him so he grabbed her face and forced her. "What did you do?"

"Don't trust her, Reece," she said as she looked into his eyes.

"What the fuck did you do?"

"I did what needed to be done. What you were too afraid to do," she said. Reece was stuck.

"You had him killed? Are you fucking kidding me?" he asked as he let go of her and backpedaled to the desk.

"I did it for us, Reece! Can't you see that? Now we..." She tried to step towards him but her body was getting weaker with each drop of blood that hit the floor. "Now we can be together. Forever, bae!"

"You're a crazy bitch!" Reece said as he leaned against the desk.

"I'm crazy for you! Now let's take that money over there and start a new life. Reece." She stepped forward and placed her bloody palms on his cheeks as she looked into his eyes. "Let's go. I told you I could be your ride or die bitch..."

Reece gave her cold look into her fading pupils. "I'd prefer the latter."

Brass busted through the already cracked open door, and ran up the stairs following the blood. His loose Timbs hopped every two steps until he made it to the stained marble second floor. He ran inside of Unc's office and paused when he saw Reece sitting behind the desk, with blood covering his face.

"Bro...they got him. I just got word. Unc is dead, bro. And Wink," Brass said as he slowly stepped forward. Reece just stared off into space as if he had really lost his mind...he had. "They shot my nigga right beside me. You hear me? We gotta-" Brass' words got stuck in his throat when he saw DeAndrea's body sprawled across the floor in the corner near the safe. She had a wound in her stomach...and one in the center of her head.

Brass looked over at Reece and saw the tears streaming from his eyes. As much as he bumped heads with the guy, and even blackmailed him, he hated to see him like that. A blind man could read the hurt that was on Reece's face, just by the thick tension that was in the room. Brass lowered his head and shook it. The Mexican Mafia had gone too far. They'd killed Wink, Unc, and took Unc's wife out in their home. Brass knew that Reece had to be hurting to see the woman whom he obviously loved laying on the floor.

"Aye, man, we are going to get through this. You hear me, fam?" Brass said as he began pacing. "Aye, tomorrow we need to meet up at the spot and sort this shit out. Like ASAP!" Brass rubbed his palms over his head in frustration. "Them niggas gotta pay for this shit! That's on God!"

Reece was still staring off into space, stoic, emotionless, as if Brass had never entered the room.

"You hear me?" Brass asked as he rushed the desk and leaned over it towards Reece. "We gotta put all that petty bullshit that we had between us to the side, fam! We are all we got now!"

Reece still didn't move an inch. He just sat there, staring off into the distance, as tears started to pour from his eyes, like rain.

Brass stepped back and figured that he'd give the man a little time alone to cope with what had gone down. This was Brass' chance to step up now. He had to. The Mexicans had to pay in blood for what they did to the organization. Brass seemed to be the only sane one left.

"I'll let you deal with this your way tonight," Brass said as he began to step back slowly with his hands in his pockets. "But tomorrow, we handle it my way. We go to war, my nigga."

Brass understood that his words were falling on deaf ears. He looked at DeAndrea one last time. She was beautiful...even with the bullet in her head. Brass smiled and left the room.

The warm tears mixed with DeAndrea's blood on Reece's cheeks. He finally moved his head as he slammed his fist on the desk in fury. He slowly opened that fist, and crinkled in his palm, was a bloody $100 bill, folded into a crane. He began to whimper in sorrow as he looked at the gun in his lap and then at DeAndrea...

Delayed Paper

Anticipation was killing Cydney. She hadn't received confirmation that the job was done and she could go back to living her life. DeAndrea had said she would call her after it was done and not hearing from her was a good sign, but was Reece okay and where did she stand with Chu-Chu?

"Hey, I was just calling to see if they made it on their trip safely."

There was a lot of screaming in the background as one of Chu-Chu's goons snapped Tonto's shoulder back in place.

"Three made the trip but there's one more that missed the flight."

Cydney's heart sped up as she wondered if Chu-Chu had found out about Reece somehow.

"Brass missed his flight and we're looking for him right now to give him his new boarding pass. That fool put Tonto in a sling, he needs a vacation."

She exhaled a sigh of relief.

"But you never answered my question. Are we good after this?"

"We're good." Chu-Chu said without an ounce of truth in his words. "Well, that is if I can keep my job."

"Your job?" Cydney didn't have a clue of what he was talking about.

"You know the dollars you throw me to make sure we keep your employees in line. Protection from the Mafia ain't free."

"How much was Tomas giving you?" she asked as she realized what he meant.

"We will talk business now that there's no middleman. But I'll be expecting a pay raise." He hung up and Cydney screamed out of anxiety. She didn't know if she could trust Chu-Chu and stay in Arizona or if she should stick to her plan of relocating, but she knew who would.

She left a note on the nightstand saying she would be back since Kyoko had decided to utilize the hotel's amenities to go swimming and made her way to Reece's house. She hadn't made it up the walkway before the door opened.

"Are you okay?"

Reece was wearing the same sports logo t-shirt and sweats he had on at their last meeting. There was a track of dried not white tears under his left eye and he looked like shit. He didn't respond.

"Reece are you okay?"

"Did you meet up with DeAndrea?"

A tear rolled down his left eye at the sound of her name. He had been crying for days, but not because she was dead, but the loss of Unc.

"Yeah, she came by the hotel with her Taser and gun," she said reliving her burnt earlobe.

"What happened?" his words rolled off his tongue like sandpaper. Although he was shedding tears, his voice was emotionless.

"She introduced herself as your girlfriend and then tortured me because she thought we were fucking. I had to tell her the truth or I'd be dead." Reece put his hand on the gun resting in the small of his back.

"Did you help her kill Unc?"

"Who's Unc?"

"Now isn't the time for you to play stupid." He freed the gun from the elastic waistband but kept it behind his back.

"Your boss? No. She said he was her husband and standing in the way of y'all being together. But she did call the killers on my phone to set it up, I'm sorry Reece."

"Where is DeAndrea?" That was the life or death determining question. If he didn't like her response, she'd be joining DeAndrea.

"I don't know. She said she would keep in contact but I haven't heard from her or the killers," she lied. "I came to you for an update. She wouldn't give me her number but she took mine."

"You don't know where she is?"

"No, Reece, I don't but we can go look for her. What aren't you telling me?"

He put the gun back under his t-shirt. He didn't believe Cydney especially after DeAndrea had warned him about her, but DeAndrea's words meant nothing after she killed Unc.

"430," Reece mumbled and Cydney wasn't sure if he was talking to her.

"430? What's happening at 430?"

"430 cranes, I added three yesterday."

"Wink, Brass, and your uncle. I'm sorry for your…"

"Don't say what you don't mean," he said cutting her off. "And Brass is still alive."

"But you said you added three…oh, Reece, I'm sorry."

Acting off her motherly instincts, she wrapped her arms around Reece and embraced him tightly. He wasn't into being comforted, but it felt good to be in her arms with her breasts resting against his pecs. It wasn't the time for him to make a sexual advancement. He needed to figure out if she was friend or foe. He wanted to get inside her head but because he didn't truly realize the type of woman DeAndrea was until he started fucking her, he felt he needed to do the same with Cydney.

He softly rubbed his chin across the top of her head and then slowly eased down until they were cheek to cheek. A gap grew between their bodies and Cydney nipples hardened to full erection. Before he could make his next move, she pressed her open lips against his and pulled him down to the floor. They looked like hungry vultures as they tore away at each other's flesh. For every nibble he laid, there was a bite she took. He was already in between her legs, fully dressed, but not for long. She tugged on his shirt trying to take it off until he got tired of her struggle and removed it himself. While he was tied in his shirt, she unbuttoned her blouse, unsnapped her bra, and then went for the strings on his elastic waistband.

"Hold up," he said reaching back and removing the gun. He emptied the clip and then threw the bullets around his house in different directions. Once he was done spotting all of their locations, he placed the gun next to her head and the last bullet by her side.

"Where's yours?"

"It's in my purse but it's not..."

"Real," he finished her sentence. "I didn't know it at first but when you sat next to me I saw the air cartridge."

She closed her eyes in embarrassment and when she opened them, she attacked him. Cydney grabbed the strings on his sweatpants so hard that the knot he made to keep them up locked. But that didn't stop her. She tried to break the string with her teeth. Reece knew it wouldn't work but for kicks, he had to watch. She was behaving as if she was thirsty for the dick and he was in the business of quenching her thirst. After she failed twice, Reece slid back and then stood to his feet.

"Let me help you out."

He grabbed a knife out of the kitchen and cut the strings. When he walked back into his entranceway, she was on her knees beckoning him to come. He had envisioned himself walking over to her and filling her mouth to capacity with his meat as his hand forced her to bob her head to his rhythm. Reece had never turned down head in his life but there was always a first. He looked at her mouth and could tell it worked wonders, but this was a business fuck. If she were as legit as she portrayed, he'd get his chance to feel her jaws of life.

There wasn't another name for what they were doing; they were fucking. The Mother Nature way, where the act of fucking looked more like two animals dancing in a fight scene in a Broadway musical. Whenever their pace slowed down to where it mirrored lovemaking, he'd flip her back over to her knees and cuff his arm under her stomach to prop her up. She had buckled and hit the carpet twice, but that just enraged the beast in him. The carpet burns on her stomach proved it. With every stroke, her butt slapped his lower stomach like a car colliding into a brick wall on repeat. They both were enjoying it, but not to the full extent, because they had the same thought in mind, *We're fucking raw.*

She wanted to stop him but the feeling was getting too good to her. And he didn't want to pull out because he felt like fuck it' it was already too late.

"You want us to be business partners…ok partner, what did you tell the Mexicans about me?" He let go of the support he allowed his arm to give and she toppled to the floor.

"I didn't tell him shit about you. Brass, Wink, and Bossman only, he don't know shit about an advisor."

She spread her knees and tooted her body up until she knew the dip in her back was perfect, and began throwing it back. Reece had to secure his footing as she caused him to stutter step back. Pushing her face down into the carpet helped to balance his weight evenly. The battle back and forth went on for twenty minutes as they shot questions back and forth to each other. When the questions were answered to Reece's satisfaction, he pulled out of her and dug his meat into the carpet to release his swimmers. When he was done, he stood up, reached for her hands, and pulled her up.

"You have your Origami theory and I have mine. But I believe both or real," she said extending her hand. "Partners?"

He was cuffing his meat with his hands because the throbbing had yet to stop. He poked out his elbow for her to shake instead.

"Partners," he repeated.

****

Kyoko had lied about going to the pool. Cydney had confined them to the room and she needed her freedom. She thought Cydney to be crazy for thinking she could bring her to a new place and only show her the four walls of a hotel room. It took a lot of persuading but in the end, she convinced Cydney to let her go swimming and Cydney wanted the break from her whining.

When she got off the elevator, Kyoko passed the door that read pool and slipped into the hotel's marketplace. She searched the t-shirt racks for the most fashionable one and settled for a pink t-shirt that read, "North Carolina" in white. There wasn't a variety in bottoms, only boys' swim shorts, so she grabbed a medium, paid for them, and jumped in a taxi. Her money was running low but she wanted to sightsee. Not like the average traveler that would want to visit the state's attractions, she wanted to check out their mall, dance, and strip clubs. When she found Golden East mall via Google, her heart was set on seeing it.

Two hours later with five bags that contained one item in it from each store, she was ready to get back to the hotel. She was surprised the stolen credit card had still worked. It had been well over a week since she slid it out of the guy's shirt pocket during her lap dance. She was sure that Cydney had checked to make sure she was in the pool by then and there would be hell to pay for her disappearance. She made her way back to the taxi and the driver popped the truck and got out of the cab. When Kyoko went to place her bags in the trunk, a freshly shot dead body and a hit to the back of her head met her.

"You know the thing about Asians in Rock City?" Brass whispered. "They stand out if they're not wearing aprons…" Brass pushed Kyoko on top of the dead body and slammed the trunk closed. He looked around, spotted a surveillance camera that was slightly pointed in his direction, and then vowed to watch the news to see if he had been seen. "That shit was easier than I thought it would be," he said to himself and drove off.

*****

Brass steered the old cab into the warehouse, the same warehouse where D-Rock had escaped and started the whirlpool that drowned so many souls. Now Wink was gone, and Unc, and Brass was left to either step up to the plate, or watch Reece strike out with a business that he knew nothing about. Brass wasn't about to let Unc's empire dwindle into crumbs under a Mexican's thumb. He would rise to the throne that he rightfully inherited, but first there was a matter of revenge. Whoever ordered the hit on Unc and Wink had to pay...in blood.

He stepped out of the car and removed his jacket. He tossed the garment to the side and flicked on the light switch. The bulb blinked a few times before it fully illuminated with a low buzzing tone that haunted the stale room. Brass lowered the garage bay and turned towards the car with a scowl. The Asian knew something, and he'd beat it out of her Hello Kitty ass if he had to.

He stuck the key into the trunk, and as soon as the latch released, Kyoko sprung forward with a crowbar, stabbing him in the chest...the same spot where D-Rock had struck him. The tool wasn't sharp enough to pierce his flesh, but it did open up an old wound, physically and emotionally. He stumbled backwards, holding his chest like Redd Foxx, as Kyoko leapt from the trunk and ran for the small door beside the bay.

She pushed with all of her might, and then pulled with as much force that her frail arms would muster, but the chain and lock laughed at her as it jangled to the soundtrack of failure. Brass regained his wits and watched her. He shook his head and pulled out a cigarette, confident that she couldn't escape.

"That's the thing about me, baby girl. I learn quickly," he said referring to how D-Rock escaped.

Kyoko turned to him, looked around, and dashed for the garage door. She yanked upwards on the bottom, but her efforts were wasted. She saw the chain for the mechanical override and tugged at it. She pulled, leaned back, and even jumped on it, letting her body weight work for her...but nothing happened.

On her last breath, she felt Brass grab her shoulders. She instantly turned around and kicked for his nuts, but he blocked it with a lucky twist of his thigh. Out of fear for her life, she released a fury of punches that landed on air until he caught her by her wrists, still holding the cigarette in his mouth as he smiled at her, and slung her body to the cement floor. The impact knocked the wind out of her, but she pounced back up like a ninja.

"Calm the fuck down!" Brass said as he pointed a pistol at her. She froze and raised her arms in surrender. "I ain't 'bout to be fighting with yo' lil' Chun Li looking ass," he said as he grabbed her and shoved her towards the car. She placed her back to it and kept her arms up.

"What do you want from me?" she asked as her lips trembled.

"I want the niggas who killed my people, and I want that bitch too," Brass said as he gripped the pistol and removed the cigarette from his lips.

"Which bitch?" Kyoko asked sincerely.

"The one who set my people up. I want that Mexican mofo since he's calling the shots. Since he's coming for my crown!"

"Oh...so you are in charge now huh? Wink mentioned your plan."

Brass dashed over and jammed the barrel of the gun against her cheek.

"Don't say my nigga's name! Ever!" He stepped back but kept his aim.

"He just said that you wanted to be king. That's all..." Kyoko said softly.

"Yeah...so what? I am now. And I'ma kill everyone you love, bitch!"

"And you'd waste no bullets..." Kyoko said with a straight face. "'Cause I don't love anybody."

Brass smiled and lowered his gun. He knew she wasn't a threat, and his arm was getting tired, it still sore from the strike.

"You're bleeding. Did I do that?"

He looked down and touched his t-shirt in the reddened area.

"Nah...Some Scars Never Heal," he said. "So you don't have any loved ones huh? I guess you some gangsta bitch, huh?" Brass asked as he sized her up from afar.

"When your family sells you off to a human trafficking organization, just to pay off your father's gambling debt, you tend to become stoic," Kyoko said as she lowered her arms now that the gun was no longer was aimed at her.

"What are you talking about?" Brass raised a brow.

"You should be careful what you wish for...King," Kyoko said as she crossed her legs and her arms.

"Oh, yeah? You think I'm scared of that Mexican fuck boy I keep hearing about?" Brass asked. "I'll. Murder. His. Whole. Fuck. Ing. Family!" Brass said as he pointed the gun with each syllable.

The room grew quiet and he let the weapon rest at his side as he wiped his face with the sleeve of his shirt.

"Have you ever heard of The Origami Theory?" Kyoko broke the silence.

"Fuck is that?" Brass asked as he began pacing with his eyes on the floor. His mind was racing and he needed an end-goal before he ran out of fuel. He had grabbed the wrong girl, but hopefully she could lead him to the right one.

"Japanese legend says if you fold 1,000 paper cranes, you'll be granted a wish." Brass gave her a confused look, wondering where the story was going. "There was a girl. Her name was Sadako. She survived the bombing on Hiroshima, but years later, she became sick with radiation poisoning. So she tested the theory on her death bed...you know...wanting that one wish." Brass couldn't help but become interested in the story as he stopped pacing and stared at her. "She did it. She made 1,000 of them hos and made her wish, just as legend promised."

"And?" Brass asked once she got quiet.

"And it worked, just as legend promised. She was healed of radiation poisoning," Kyoko said with a forced smile. "Then she died the next week of leukemia," Kyoko said as she let her arms drop to her side and grinned.

"That's some fucked up shit to smile about," Brass said.

"I say that to say this, be careful what you wish for...King."

"You think I can't handle it? You think I'm scared of Choo-choo train or whatever the fuck-boy name is? That's what you think huh? You are going to lead me to that bitch that you work for, and then she will lead me to his ass. I'll cut the head of the snake off and then let the tail slither into the grass. He's no king! I run this city, you hear me?" Brass said as he beat his chest. Kyoko started laughing. "The fuck is funny?" Her laughter increased in octaves.

"You are," she said in between catching her breath. "You think Chu-Chu is the head of the snake? Noooooo Chu-Chu is just the rattle. Cydney is the fangs!"

"What?" Brass asked as he stepped closer.

"Yes. She set all this up. Don't shit shake without her giving approval for it. You are worthless to her. You aren't even worth the brass that encases the bullet she'll use to kill you. Reece is the only one she values...and once their partnership blossoms, you'll see how little you are in the grand scheme of things."

"What do you mean their partnership?" Brass asked as he stepped in her face. "Reece had something to do with all of this? Tell me that nigga didn't set my people up!" Brass barked.

"That's for you to find out." Brass' jaw tightened and he wanted to punch her lights out, but she had just proven how valuable she truly was. "In his defense, I don't think he knew that he was kissing the devil...her poison is more of an aftertaste." Kyoko grinned as she licked her lips seductively.

"She always gets her man." Brass snatched her up by the collar of the cheap gift shop shirt and tossed her into the passenger seat of the cab. She screamed as he slammed the door behind her, almost catching her leg.

"Where are we going?"

"To get our man…"

 Sands of Time

The day had evolved into night and Cydney was still lying comfortably in Reece's arms. They spent the entire day discussing their business venture in between business fucks. In twelve hours, she knew she didn't want to spend another day on Earth without Reece by her side. He was intelligent; college educated, and had exceptional street smarts. Maybe it was the sore spot in between her legs thinking for her, but she was feeling like Reece was the one. Not meaning the one she'd stand with in front of a pastor, but a lifelong business partner with perks. Her grandfather had branded in her head that everything happened for a reason when she questioned life, and now it had finally made sense.

"You call the hotel to check on your girl yet?" He had been combing his fingers through her hair for the past five minutes.

"Not in a few hours. Can you hand me my phone please, business partner?"

The phone was under the wreckage their clothes made on her side of the bed on the floor.

"Partner, not slave. You can get your shit yourself." He raised his chest lifting her head off it and got out of the bed. Cydney smiled as he walked to her side of the bed and then frowned as he walked past her phone. She wanted to chop it up to him having mixed emotions, but the truth was he hadn't displayed any emotions to her besides lust.

The phone rang three times and then forwarded her call back to the front desk.

"I'm sorry ma'am, your party isn't answering."

"Thank you." She hung up the call and dialed Kyoko's cell phone but it was still going straight to voicemail.

"Did she answer?" Reece walked back into the room holding two tall glasses of orange of juice.

"No, I'm starting to think she caught a flight back home. She isn't built like us, this was too much for her to handle."

He handed her a glass.

"Naw, somebody got to her. Brass isn't smart enough to come up with a plan without Wink but the Mexicans are. Didn't you say they knew what hotel you were staying in?"

"Should I call them?"

"Hell no and I guess you're staying here tonight because I'm sure they have somebody waiting for you to return." Reece walked over to the pile and sorted through the clothing until he retrieved all of his.

"Get dressed, we'll go grab something to eat and get a hotel room. Your Asian friend knows where I live; we are no longer safe."

She put on her clothes as Reece grabbed his already packed suitcase, the duffle bag of money, and an empty trash bag to put his cranes in. Once Cydney was dressed, she helped him fill the trash bag. The money cranes were beautiful but the blood behind them would leave a stain, and for the first time that day, she began to question the ideal of going into partnership with him. He had made a bad decision when he let her live in the VIP room. If he had killed her, none of this would be happening. Not to mention the fact he had been fucking his boss's wife. What mistakes would he make working with Cydney and how would he stab her in the back? She couldn't sleep on the facts and she wouldn't.

"Maybe we shouldn't go into hiding together, what if they find us? We're both dead."

"Then we go out like partners." He placed the last crane in the bag.

"But we aren't officially partners yet."

"Not officially partners? What the fuck are you..." He stopped talking. "You're right...we're not official." That was all he said but he wanted to say more. They had spent twelve hours mapping out their plan and fucking raw without a care in the world, and then Cydney declared them unofficial partners. He didn't know what she had up her sleeve but if she wanted to make it in the traps Rock City set by herself, he wouldn't try to stop her. Reece snatched her cellphone out of her hand and programed his number in it. It was different from the one she originally had.

"It's a message line. Leave one when you're ready to move forward with things."

He returned the phone to its owner, grabbed her purse, and rushed her to the door. She was trying to say something to him but he wasn't in the mood to listen. He was too busy fighting the urge to kill her and wanted her to leave so he wouldn't have the option to. The business plan was nice but the sex and personal conversation was better. If she was really the person who laid on his chest reciting her goals and the in-depth structure of her origami theory, then Reece had just spent the day fucking his future wife. However, she wasn't displaying that goal driven woman at the moment. Her face read, don't trust me because I don't trust you, and he was thankful he was literate.

In the past few days, his world had been flipped upside down like a kid bullied by life. He just hung there and watched as his lunch money fell to the surface, just out of his reach in the cafeteria of fate. Unc was a great mentor, and the only father figure that Reece had ever known. He owed his life to him, and part of his after life in that debt. Then there was the fog of losing DeAndrea. He claimed that he didn't love her, and it was just a fuck, but in the end he got fucked, discarded, and left feeling used by life and sexually assaulted by the gritty hands of karma. Finally, there was Wink. He was a loyal soldier, loyal to Brass, but loyal nonetheless. Reece couldn't relax around the new face, the devil in a pretty dress. What if she was up to something and had a deadly ulterior motive? Or worse…what if he fell in love and then lost her like he did DeAndrea…what if he was forced to 'lose' her, and make another crane? These questions plagued him so he defended his heart with brashness.

"Reece, maybe we should stick together," she said as he opened the door for her. "I mean, I don't know the city. Where will I go, what will I do?"

He chuckled feeling like the dude from 'Gone with the Wind' as he spoke,

"Shit… frankly Cydney, I give no fucks." He slammed the door in her face and waited for her to pull off before getting in his car and doing the same.

*****

Brass drove to one of his stash houses, well it was his now that Unc had met his demise, and pulled around back. Kyoko rode silently for the most part and just stared out the window; that trait reminded Brass of his late homie Wink. He was always a quiet dude and very observant- if only he could've reacted quicker when the Reaper rolled up. That was cool though, Brass had a plan to bring the Reaper to his Mexican knees, and choke him with a brass rosary.

Once they were around the back of the house, Brass instructed her to follow him as he hopped into a black Honda Accord. It was his getaway vehicle if shit ever hit the fan, and feces were definitely striking the blades now…but he had no intentions of running.

"Hurry, girl. We have a lot of shit to do…partna."

"What is your plan, Brass? You think you are going to go head up with the Mexican Mafia solo?" she asked as she climbed inside. "I mean, I can hold my own, no-fucking-doubt, but still…we are outnumbered."

Brass pulled out a blunt and gave it a lick over for good measures. Kyoko just looked at him, waiting for a response or some form of acknowledgement to her inquiry.

"Listen, little girl. Let me do the thinking. You just sit over there and look pretty, ok?" he said as he fired up the blunt and threw the car in reverse.

"You think I'm pretty?" Kyoko asked as she animatedly batted her eyes and leaned on his shoulder. He forcefully shrugged her away with annoyance as she broke into laughter. She was working his nerves and derailing his train of thought, so he turned on the music. As soon as the tunes hit, she reached over and twisted the knob off. Brass was about to reenact a scene from Rush Hour on her ass.

"You listen to Drake?"

"Yeah, why?" he asked.

"I dunno...just weird, ya know?"

Brass pulled the blunt and blew smoke out of the window.

"How so? What's wrong with Drake?" The weed was relaxing him so he figured that he would entertain her in small talk.

"I mean, you supposed to be this big macho killer, and you in here listening to Drake sing and shit," she said as she broke out into laughter again. Her laugh was annoying but contagious- still Brass couldn't crack a smile. "You supposed to be in here listening to some fucking Wu-Tang or something."

"The fuck yo' young ass know about Wu-Tang?" Brass asked as he sized her up. She couldn't have been older than 19.

"What?" She reached into her pocket and pulled out her cellphone. She snatched the auxiliary cord from his phone like she was pulling the plug on a vacuum cleaner from down the hall. "Peep this shit, my nigga," she said as the tunes blared and she started rocking her body in a gangsta impression. She folded her arms in a B-Boy stance and pretended to grab a mic. "Pass the blunt!" she said as she pointed at it in Brass' fingertips. He was about to until he realized that she was rapping the lyrics. Brass had to crack a smile at the act, and the gesture felt good to the tense muscles in his face. She was putting on a show and she broke out into laughter as she turned the music back down.

"Girl, you crazy as fuck," he said as he flicked the roach out the window. "Oh, and by the way. I don't think you can say the word nigga..." The humor vanished from her face as she stared a hole into his jaw.

"And you can because your people were slaves? Fuck outta here. 'I was a slave. I still am. You ain't experienced shit until you've been a sex slave; you feel that? And a slave of lust, or a slave of labor, is the same crop...my nigga," Kyoko said as she folded her arms and went back to staring out the window.

They rode in silence for a while with no destination in particular, and Kyoko picked up on it.

"Dude, you can't go at Chu-Chu on your own."

"I still have troops in these streets. Don't worry your little sweet ass."

"Still...maybe you should play this smart. I have a plan."

Brass looked over at her with a puzzled expression.

"What's that?"

She slowly turned her head to him and grabbed his hand. He tried to remain focused on the road as she started sucking his fingers, lubing his skin with her saliva. Just as his dick was about to wake up and pay attention, at attention, she slid his brass knuckles off. "The fuck you doing, girl?"

She held the brass knuckles up and smiled at him.

"We make them think that you are dead..."

*****

Chu-Chu and his men sat on the porch of the rusted trailer as the black Honda pulled into the driveway. Tonto hopped off the porch with his arm in a sling and approached the driver's side of the car with a pistol in his good hand. He stepped back as Kyoko stepped out and gave him the elevator look. She had changed clothes and was now sporting a short schoolgirl ruffled skirt and a white blouse. Her hair was tied into two cliché ponytails with pink ribbons that matched her pink stockings.

"Chu-Chu, I have a gift for you, holmes!" she said as she ignored Tonto and applied a fake accent.

"Shit, it better be some of that tight Asian pussy," Tonto said as he drooled over her. "I heard that Asian pussy taste like duck sauce..." Kyoko frowned from disgust.

"The fuck kinda pussy you eating that taste like duck sauce?"

"Tonto! Get your crippled ass away from her!" Chu-Chu barked as he descended the steps. Tonto did as he was ordered, but not before holding up the peace sign and flickering his tongue between it.

"Getcho ass back. Don't you know if you eat Chinese pussy, vato, you'll be right back hungry in 10 minutes?"

"I'm Japanese, bitch," Kyoko said as she rolled her eyes. She popped the trunk with the key fob and escorted him to the rear of the car. "It is a gift, from Cydney," Kyoko said as she pointed to the burned corpse in the trunk…similar to the one that she was lying on hours earlier, fearing for her own life. Now she was in control, and it felt marvelous.

"Who is this?" Chu-Chu asked as he looked at the charred body that was beyond recognition.

Kyoko reached in, grabbed the brittle hand, and held it up. The seared Brass knuckles told it all. Chu-Chu stepped back with a smile as he rubbed his chin.

"So are we good?" she asked as she closed the trunk and leaned on it.

"And you ladies did what my soldiers couldn't huh?" Chu-Chu asked as he glanced back at Tonto.

"We have our ways…"

"Hmmm," Chu-Chu said as he continued to rub his chin.

"The city is yours, boss man. Do with it what you please," Kyoko said as she strutted to the driver's side and climbed in. As she was closing the door, Chu-Chu leaned in.

"Tell Cydney to stay close. I never know when I may need another favor," he said as he patted the roof of the car and turned to his men. He put his hands on his hips as he briefed them while Kyoko disappeared down the driveway. "Prepare for stage two of the Spanish Invasion…"

Back to Alpha

Reece had driven around Unc's subdivision like a lost tourist. With every pass of the driveway that led to Unc's house, the yellow police tape woven through the gate brought him to tears. He didn't want to be alone at that moment, nor did he need to. He thought about hitting up Shawna, the girl he had been hitting from time to time, but she wasn't the company he needed. She was a cum guzzler and after the fiasco he had with Cydney all day, he knew couldn't wet her whistle nor provide enough for her to guzzle.

Reece had a few places he could lay low but Unc had furnished them to him and with the feds more than likely involved with Rock City king pin's double homicide, the houses were now off limits to him too. He pulled out his cell phone and looked up hotels more than an hour's drive away and his text message alert went off.

"I'm sorry, please come to me."

"Who is this?" he texted back using predictive texting.

"We got this number out of Wink's phone, partner."

Sirens went off in his head and Cydney had just ran out of passes. Her bullshit had finally made it to his nose and he recognized the scent, she was playing him. Before she left his house, he'd given her a message line number and he had texted back in forth with her on his trap phone. Why wouldn't she speak up and say that she already had his personal cell phone number? All that meant to him was that she was keeping secrets. Yet the question remained, what secrets was she hiding? He pulled up at the gas station he agreed to meet her at and she was at the pump filling up.

"Look, I don't know what's going on but I just got a thank you call from the Mexicans for bring them Brass' body. He said something about Kyoko delivering him to them. I've been trying to call her but her phone is still going to voicemail." She placed the pump back in the slot that housed the nozzle. "We got our chance; we have one shot for a do over. Are you going to use it with me?"

"It's been a long ass day; I need you to get to the point." Exhaustion was taking over him and if he didn't get to a pillow fast, he'd fall asleep standing on his feet.

"Arizona, we hit the road now. I'll drive until I get sleepy and once we are across state lines, we'll check in to a hotel, and get some rest."

"You want me to go along with your flow and step out on faith…on you?"

"You have faith in making those stupid cranes." The words slipped off her tongue. "I didn't mean to call them stupid but you don't know if you'll get your wish once you reach 1000 or not, but you're still folding those bitches. All I'm asking is for you to do the same with me. If it doesn't work, you're free to go."

His eyelids closed at her last words. Her mouth was moving but nothing was coming out of it that he understood. He could feel Cydney moving around him quickly but his mind had already called it a night.

"Here," she said snapping him out of it by handing him his bag. "Unfold these while I drive, no one is going to die due to our partnership." He put the bag in her trunk and was shocked to see she had already placed his other bags in there.

"I'm going to hold on to them a little bit longer. Go in there and get an energy shot, I'm driving! There's no way a city girl like you will make it out these woods this time of night without hitting a deer."

"Please, you were just sleep on your feet. I'll make it."

"I know you're use to running the Cydney show but if you're fucking with me, your show just got cancelled. If I say I'm good, then I'm good. Now go grab two of them."

She rolled her eyes but did as she was told. She had called him sleepy but she was snoring before they got out of the city's limits. Reece didn't stop to get a hotel until they made it to a suburban area outside of Nashville, Tennessee.

"Wake up, go get us a room with a double bed."

Cydney filled her lungs with air and screamed as loud as she could. She was at the punchline of the nightmare she was having and although she felt awake, the bad guy from her dream was staring her in the face."

"Why in the fuck are you screaming?"

He looked around to see if she had grabbed anyone's attention and like a bloodhound, the valet had his eyes locked on them. He put his walkie-talkie to his mouth for a few seconds and two men came running out of the automatic doors of the hotel. They huddled up around the valet as if he was a quarterback on the fourth down going for the first. Once the valet yelled break, all three men approached the vehicle.

"Go meet them halfway. When they ask you why you screamed like that tell them a cicada flew in the car."

"A cia- what?"

"A cicada. Now go!"

She didn't have a clue what Reece was talking about but if she wanted him to trust her, she'd have to show that she trusted him. She darted out the car and met the men 100 feet away from it.

"I'm sorry for screaming but a cicada flew in the car."

"Every 13 years I wished I lived somewhere else. The don't bite but they'll stick to you and the noise will drive you insane," the only black face in the group of red-coated men said. He held his index finger to his lips and her ears turned on. There was a loud irritating buzz vibrating in her ears that sent a chill down her spine and caused her to shiver.

"Are you checking in? Need us to help grab your bags?" the original valet on the scene asked. She looked over shoulder at the car and saw Reece was carrying all of them.

"No, he's a typical man. He's going carry all those bags in now because he'd be damned if he's making another trip."

She exited the conversation with a laugh and was at the front desk before Reece made it in.

"And can we have a 9am wakeup call?"

"Make that 10am, its 6 now," Reece said to the desk agent.

He had told her to get a double room but since they were getting shelter on her dollar, she booked a studio suite instead. Reece jumped in the shower while Cydney stripped down to her birthday suit and got in bed. The fatty meat between her thighs was sore to the touch from the beating Reece put on it hours earlier but she still wanted more. She hadn't been fucked without feelings being involved in years and she was enjoying it. When the water cut off in the restroom she rolled the covers down until her breasts were kissed by the warmth of the room and pretended to be asleep. In her mind, she was being sexy and there was no way Reece would be able to lay next to her naked body and not touch it, she was exactly right. When he saw her nipples sitting hard in the air the elevator turned on his boxers. He walked over to her with lust flowing through his blood and his mouth watering with each step he took towards the peak of her mountains. It took every ounce of strength he had in him to not dip down and place one of them in his mouth as he reached for the extra pillows. He made himself a small fort on the floor with the pillows and then laid on his stomach until his steel reverted back to its norm.

"Why are you on the floor? If you don't want to sleep next to me that's fine, we can lay head to toe but I feel totally disrespected with you on that floor!"

"You feel disrespected and I feel like I'm walking into a trap. We're both fucked up, now go to sleep."

"I haven't done anything for you to feel like I'm trying to set you up. But those are your feelings so keep your pink ass on the floor then!"

Horny was turning into angry quickly and although the words came out of her lips, it was the lips between her legs fueling her words.

"You're alive because I didn't snitch on you!"

"So you're saying you snitched on Unc?" He was in her face before she knew he was coming. "You set up Unc?" Dehydrated spit formed in the corners of his mouth like a pit-bull.

"No, your bitch set him up and if you loved this Unc so much then why was your dog ass fucking his wife? You think I'm setting you up and I'm starting to feel the same way. If you'd stab your boss that you loved and adored in the back how in the fuck am I not supposed to feel like you won't do the shit to me?"

He was mad but she was right, Reece did bite the hand that fed him. Unc had raised him never to put any weight into hos and he watched him fuck whatever female he wanted to in the city with his wedding ring in his pocket. However, if Unc didn't respect his own marriage why should he?

"So now you don't trust me because I'm not trying to give you this dick, is that what this is about?"

"Don't answer my questions with a question. If you loved him then why were you fucking his bitch?" she said feeling like Kyoko as she rolled her eyes.

"Because of the same reason you didn't tell me you had my personal number back at my house, it was business. You had to make sure your ducks were in a row and so did I. They were business fucks, the same business fucks I gave you." Reece sat down on the bed. "That's all it was."

"Hell naw, that bitch was in love with you."

"And you will fall in love with me too," he shouted over her words and she didn't have a rebuttal ready to shoot back at him. "That's why I didn't give you this dick. I sealed our business deal with a nut and now that we're officially partners, you're cut off."

He meant what he said when he said it but once her jaws locked around his shaft, the white flag went up as he ate his words. The business fuck had turned into a soul tie as he drank her natural fluids in a 69 position. He even made the mistake of marking his spot as his unprotected explosion entered her welcoming wound. Reece had fallen asleep with his shrinking meat fighting to stay inside of her. He was too sleepy to worry about the consequences of his actions.

******

"Are you sure they bought it?" Brass asked as he walked through the living room of the vacant trailer. Kyoko was standing in the kitchen with her hands on her hips as she stared at him with confidence.

"Of course…it's called Asian Persuasion," she said as she grabbed her laptop from the counter.

There was a small card table in the corner of the living room, so she decided to set up shop there. She found a white bed sheet from the bedroom and two nails from the laundry closet. Brass sat near the front window and peeked out of the tatty blinds with his index finger. He had found the perfect hideout spot, a vacant trailer four spots down from where Chu-Chu and his men had planted their headquarters. He had the perfect view to keep an eye on them and their activities, as he waited patiently for the perfect moment to strike.

"If you are hiding from them, you sure picked the dumbest spot to do it," Kyoko said as she hung the white sheet on the wall behind the small table, using her heels as a hammer to nail the curtain in place.

"Keep your enemies close..." Brass said as he turned to her and fired up a cigarette. He was wondering what she was up to. She pulled the chair back and opened up her laptop, as the bright screen seemed to illuminate the dim room. Then she activated the mobile Wi-Fi hotspot on her cellphone. After a few keystrokes, she was adjusting the screen for the perfect angle as she slid her chair from side to side in different poses.

"You sure take that Queen of the Selfie shit to heart, huh?" Brass asked, merely making small talk to kill time. She was no longer his prisoner, and had ample opportunity to escape, but she came back. Maybe they were after the same thing, revenge to a boss who wronged them.

"This is deeper than selfies," she said as she smiled into the webcam and jiggled her cleavage. "I host live webcam shows for a site called PornHuddy. It's like PornHub but only better," she said as she adjusted her two ponytails.

Brass was intrigued at the many avenues the girl had for getting money. Maybe they could partner up after the fiasco settled. He shook his head at the crazy thought and focused back out the window. His main goal now was getting his streets back, and not letting some Mexican move in on his inherited territory. The immigrants weren't about to steal his job...

The sound of exaggerated sucking caught Brass' attention as he turned towards Kyoko. She had a large black dildo in her hand and sucked on it for the webcam. Her skill was evident as she skated her tongue around the tip as if she was carving an ice sculpture. Brass felt his dick jump but turned back to the window. A few of Chu-Chu's men were loading some bags in the back of a black Suburban, making multiple trips leaving the backdoor to the vehicle ajar.

"I thought you despised being a sex slave?" Brass asked as he pulled on the cigarette.

"I do, but we do what we must, right?" she said without even looking at him. She slid the dildo down her chest as she pulled out her large breasts and massaged her perky nipples with the tip of the dildo. The binging sound from the chatroom of her viewers echoed in the room as they each took turns typing out requests. "But as entertainers we are always a slave to the people. No matter if you are an actor, a musician, or even an author...the audience owns you. That's what they pay for."

Brass didn't hear shit she said. He was busy licking his lips at the show himself. He shook his head and tried to focus out the window again but her moans grabbed his ears like an angered stepmom. He looked over and she had slid her chair back and was now fucking herself slowly with the dildo. Her head tilted back with her legs arched on the table as the black shaft slid in and out of her lubricated canal. Before he knew it, Brass was on his feet and walking over with his homing erection leading the way.

"Can I join?" Brass asked as he dropped the cigarette and stepped on it with the sole of his boot. Kyoko opened her eyes and smiled at him.

"You sure you want to be in the entertainment business?" Brass nodded like a child being offered candy by a blacked out van. She leaned forward and started typing. "I have to ask the people," she said with a seductive grin. "They said yeah." Before her words even escaped her lips, Brass' jeans escaped his hips, and now his dick was protruding into the camera angle.

"Oh no, nobody gets to fuck this pussy," she said as she waved her finger in a disciplinary fashion. "They want you to eat it..." Brass was taken aback. He leaned back like she swung at him.

"Hell no! I don't eat no pussy!"

"Then go back to your window...like a pussycat," Kyoko taunted as she licked her two fingers and inserted them into her walls. Brass took a deep swallow and dropped to his knees. He got in position, but she pulled him closer with her legs on his shoulder, breaking his hesitation, and mushing his face into her mush. He tried to pull back, but her moans were enchanting.

Fuck it...

He started licking her box like a cautious kitten being given a bowl of milk from a stranger. Gently his tongue poked her wet hole and at first, he frowned at the taste, but once she grabbed the back of his head, he was all in it. He found himself enjoying being dominated by his Asian captor. My-my, had the tables turned.

"Suck the clit..." Kyoko purred. Brass didn't like that, because his mentality led him to comparing it to sucking dick, but he did it anyways. The binging from the chatroom was going haywire with requests. She grabbed the back of his head and grinded his face into her box as he sucked on her clit like the first slurp of a milkshake through a straw. Finally, she stood up and instructed him to sit down on the floor and lean his head back on the chair. It was uncomfortable, but he did it...for the people.

She squatted over his face and landed her pussy on the landing strip that he called a tongue. First with slow grinds, but as she felt her climax reaching its climax, she rolled her orgasmic eyes and danced on his face like a teen hunching a pillow. Her juices covered his face like a pie-eating contest, and to the victor went the spoils.

"Let me hit..." Brass said as he stood up. Kyoko went back to typing as if nothing ever happened. She knew that she now had control over him. He was her sex slave now.

"Nope. Not until you have proven yourself worthy." Brass frowned but played the game anyway.

"And how can I do that?" he asked. Without even looking, she pointed at the window.

"Go kill Chu-Chu, and I'll let you fuck this pussy." Brass turned to the window, grabbed his coat and his pistol, and stormed out the back door. Kyoko smiled at the power she had just instilled as she leaned back in the chair. She folded her arms behind her head and chuckled.

"Pussy-a-do-it…"

*****

The black Suburban coasted through the back streets that led from Sharpsburg to the city limits of Rock City. Tonto was steering the wheel with one arm. Chu-Chu lounged in the passenger as Latin rap bumped through the speakers. The roads were dark and vacant, surrounded by trees and open fields during the stretch, making a tranquil backdrop for the immigrant thugs.

"Beautiful isn't it?" Chu-Chu asked as he glanced out the window at the passing trees. Tonto glanced over at him and shook his head as he adjusted his short statue in the seat.

"If you say so. Too country for me. Too dark. I need lights."

"It's peaceful here. I may move the family out here and settle down you know. Go fishing and shit with the kids," Chu-Chu said as he rubbed his chin deep in thought.

"Whatever. Let's just get this money first before you start talking about retirement," Tonto said as he put the vehicle on cruise control. He leaned back and folded his arm behind his head. "It is peaceful though. I'll give you that."

"This city is wide open space for the taking. Their king is gone and the streets are starving. That's why when we meet up with these blacks tonight; we need to play it cool. They will try and negotiate, but remember that we have the upper hand…we have the dope."

"True," Tonto commented as he steered with his knees. "The boys loaded it all in the back. Should be a simple ride." Chu-Chu looked over at him and pointed.

"Nothing is as simple as it seems. Don't underestimate these people. The ride is easy now, but remember to always keep your eyes on the road. You got me?" Chu-Chu dropped the jewel. Tonto nodded and grabbed the wheel as he sat upwards. Something moved in the back catching their attention. Brass tumbled over the third row seat and landed with a pistol to the side of Tonto's head. Before either one of them could react, Brass pulled the hammer back with a scowl.

"Or end up road kill," Brass said. Tonto reached for his hip but Brass pulled the trigger, painted the front windshield with his brains and blood. Tonto's body slumped forward and the pistol turned to Chu-Chu who was frozen in place as the vehicle continued to cruise-uncontrollably.

"You look like you've seen a ghost," Brass said as he rested the hot barrel on his temple. Chu-Chu grabbed the wheel and tried to keep the vehicle steady on the road to the best of his ability, due to half of the windshield being dyed burgundy and pink. Tonto's deadweight was countering the direction that Chu-Chu was trying to lead the vehicle.

"Sucks to see your man die right beside you huh?" Brass asked, referring to seeing Wink take his last breath in the passenger seat.

"They said you were dead...I saw the body..." Chu-Chu tried to remain calm. His eyes cut to Tonto's waist where the butt of his gun was barely visible. He had to come up with a plan and quickly, before Brass made art on his side of the windshield.

"The best trick the devil ever pulled was making the world think that he didn't exist," Brass recited with a grin. He was enjoying seeing Chu-Chu shiver under his power.

"The bitch lied to me. She's a snake, can't you see that. She set all of us up. We need to be working together, brother…"

Brass chuckled. "Brother? My nigga, ain't shit about us kin, you feel me?" Chu-Chu was still keeping the vehicle stable as they entered city limits. The streetlights welcomed them, but he knew that eventually they would hit traffic, or a turn.

"That's where you are wrong. We are both two lost souls trying to survive a car wreck…" Brass raised a brow just as Chu-Chu snatched the wheel. Not wearing a seat belt, Brass' body was slung against the window as the tires of the Suburban drew smoke. The vehicle slid sideways down the neighborhood street just inside of the city as Chu-Chu reached over and grabbed Tonto's pistol while fighting against gravity and momentum.

Brass fired off a wild shot as he tried to sit up, but the vehicle tilted to its side, crashing his head against the window again, this time shattering it. The vehicle slid down the asphalt sending sparks into the air like a failed firework that went astray. The seatbelt held Chu-Chu in place and he fired a shot into Brass' shoulder just before the vehicle collided into a SUV and spun into a pole.

Chu-Chu blacked out for a minute but snapped back to his senses with his face smothered into the airbag. He undid his seatbelt and looked for Brass. He wasn't there, but blood and cloth lined the broken window where his body had been. He must have been thrown from the vehicle when they collided with the SUV. Chu-Chu climbed out and limped around the wreckage, looking for Brass. He saw him sprinting with an injured bop yards away and disappeared behind some houses. Chu-Chu had a decision to make. Leave his dope and chase after Brass, or stay back and clean up the mess before the police came. The decision was made for him when a studious looking white man walked over to him from the damaged SUV.

"You ok?" the man asked as he held his own bruised forehead. He stood in front of Chu-Chu and pulled out his cellphone. "Just have a seat. I'll call the police. It's going to be ok, buddy," he said as he turned his back to Chu-Chu and put the phone to his ear.

"No, don't call the police," Chu-Chu said as he forced himself to stand up straight, ignoring the pain in his ribs. "I said don't!" Chu-Chu screamed, but the man was busy on the phone...leaving Chu-Chu no choice. He pulled Tonto's pistol and fired a shot into the back on the man's head. The noble citizen fell forward, lifeless, as his blood spilled across the asphalt mixing with the debris of the wreckage. Chu-Chu stomped the cellphone with his heel and shook his head.

"Fucking white people always flirt with death." He looked at the man's vehicle and noticed that it was still drivable, so he loaded his dope in the back of it, and drove back to headquarters.

~

Kyoko shook her head when she peeked out of the blinds and saw Chu-Chu pull up to his hangout clearly banged up but still alive-Tonto wasn't with him though. Just then, the back door burst open, and in limped Brass. He was bleeding badly from his shoulder with cuts all over his body. He staggered towards Kyoko and collapsed right at her feet, breathing heavily.

"I see you missed the main target," she said coldly.

"I tried…he was…he was…he was too slippery this time," Brass said as his consciousness started to fade. Kyoko shook her head knowing that she would have to stitch him up and save his life if he was to continue to be somewhat useful.

"And to think, you wanted to fuck this pussy," she taunted as she stepped over him.

*****

"Chu! What happen, Holmes?" his crew ran up to him and helped him inside the trailer and to a couch. They all crowded around him as he waved his hand for breathing space.

"Move!" he barked as he tried to catch his breath. "Bring me that bitch, Cydney!" he commanded. One of his men stepped forward with a dumb look on his face.

"Oh, I meant to tell you. Word came through the pipeline. She and her peeps are back in Arizona." Chu-Chu squinted his eyes and sat forward with the pistol in his hand.

"And you are just now telling me this, why?" he asked through gritted teeth. The man shrugged.

"I didn't think it was important, Holmes…"

POW!

Chu-Chu shot him right in the chest as everyone stepped back and watched their comrade stumble to the wall and buckle over. The room grew quiet as they all turned their heads slowly to their heartless leader. "Anybody else has any important info that they need to tell me?" he asked as he waved the pistol.

"Si…" a small guy with a tank top and a black bandana tired around his neck stepped forward. "Tomorrow is Tonto's birthday…"

Chu-Chu closed his eyes and released a heavy sigh.

"Pack up. We are going back to Arizona," he said as he rocked forward to his feet. "This bitch gotta die!"

Homestead

Arizona was hotter than Reece had remembered from his last visit. Cydney offered her pool to him before she left for work, but judging by the heat, he felt he would be diving into a Jacuzzi without the whirlpool jets. It was the fourth day she had locked him away in the house. She had returned the rental car to the airport but there were two cars not being used in her garage and she didn't offer him their keys. It didn't take long for Reece to realize Cydney was a control freak. She had made it obvious when she tried to force him to eat on her schedule. He almost felt like a child rebelling when he called a cab to pick him up and take him to the only place he knew of in the city, Donks Strip Club. Reece needed a drink and to checkout Cydney's setup for himself. She mentioned she had to go collect when she clocked out at 5 o'clock and then they'd have dinner at her favorite Mexican restaurant. Instead of playing prisoner until she returned, he decided to meet her there.

The club was packed for three in the afternoon and walking into it had become an issue.

"Say excuse me vato!"

Reece had bumped into an overly confident cholo who was leaving the club with his chest poked out, but it wasn't him telling him to excuse himself. A tall cat wearing a cowboy hat was flexing for him.

"My bad," Reece said nonchalantly.

"I know it's your bad, bitch. Next time you see Chu-Chu walking out you clear the way. Understood?"

So this is the infamous Chu-Chu, Reece thought as he hurriedly looked at him before he got in the backseat of a black Tahoe. He didn't look like he was the cat running the city, but history had proven he was.

"Understood," he said paying his entrance to the club and walking in.

Spanish hip-hop was playing but the majority of the club's guests were black or white.

"Sorry about that y'all, I had one of those marathon requests I couldn't say no to. Now that they are gone, let's get it back live in this bitch. Next up on the main stage is the Queen of the Selfie herself. Let's make some noise for the biggest ass and tits we've ever seen on an Asian, welcome to the stage our girl KYOKO!"

Kyoko stepped on stage in an all-black men's suit with a black driver's hat on as the beat to 'Partition' by Beyoncé came on. As the lyrics dropped, she flung the hat to the floor like she was dealing cards and dropped low pussy popping. She was left in a lace two-piece before the chorus came in. With her back to the audience, she jiggled her butt one cheek at a time and looked over her shoulder at the drooling watchers. When she saw Reece, she turned the heat up on her routine and removed the rest of her clothes. She ended her show sliding upside down slowly on the poll with her legs spread eagle showing off all her sushi.

"You liked my show?" she asked Reece when she returned from calling Brass. Kyoko needed to keep Reece there until he arrived and she thought flirty conversation would do it.

It hadn't been her day. When she walked in the club, the club owner looked at her and quickly told her to hide. Chu-Chu was hunting and she and Cydney were in season. So she had spent the hour before her performance hiding in a stall in the men's restroom. She knew it would be the last place Chu-Chu would send his guards to look and the men's suit and loafers she was wearing helped her look the part.

She didn't have an ear to the street but she knew Chu-Chu had a near death match with Brass and he would want her dead for betraying him.

"Yeah, you did your thing," Reece chuckled.

"So why you don't tip me? I killed Brass, you should have made it rain."

"Speaking of that, what happened?"

Kyoko straddled his lap cowboy style and placed her lips to his ear.

"He kidnapped me and took me to some dark warehouse. He lied and said if I got out of the chair, somebody hiding in the cut would shoot me. I was like bitch please; if someone was there with a gun, they wouldn't be hiding. So when he went to get the matches to go with the gasoline he had, I got up and grabbed the jug. He walked in, I poured it on him, and he burned to death."

"You took the matches from him too?"

"No," she said putting her hand under her skirt. "I smoke weed all day, I always keep fire on me." She revealed a Bic she had stashed in her stash.

"Damn, girl, what else do you got in there?" He laughed and shook his head in disbelief.

"Wouldn't you like to know, if you buy a private in the VIP room, I'll let you dig in there and find out yourself. You might find one of those cranes you like."

"That's what I'm afraid of," he said with a smile on his face.

One of the items on Reece's bucket list was to fuck the lining out of an Asian chick, but Kyoko didn't meet his qualifications. He knew Brass was a dumb fuck up but there was no way in hell she killed him that easily unless he had experimented with a new drug and had lost his mind.

"So we go to the VIP room now, Bossman?"

"I'll pass this time. I'm kinda here on business."

"You here to collect the money?" She handed him her $200.00 with a frown. "Here you go."

"How long have you been back?" he asked taking the money.

"Yesterday morning, I had class and then I came here."

"Oh ok, then that means you're short $200.00." He extended his hand to wait on his payment. "And show me who else I should be collecting from."

Kyoko got off his lap and walked over to an older Mexican man who was talking to the DJ. She interrupted their conversation and eventually started pointing at Reece. Taking his gun from under his shirt, Reece took it off safety, and pointed it at the man walking his way. There was something missing from the story of Brass' death, and until he figured it out, Kyoko wouldn't be trusted.

"Hello Bossman, Cydney didn't tell me she hired someone to take Tomas' place so quickly. Please follow me to the back to collect your money."

Reece left the safety off and followed the man so closely that his breath made the hairs on his neck stand up.

"This is the dressing room and no one has paid since Friday. All of the girls whose lockers have a star on them belong to you." He pulled out a key ring. "I haven't made a copy yet so when you are done collecting, please return them. The numbers on the lockers are on the keys and do me a favor, don't come back. Those Mexicans want Cydney's operation here shutdown. They told me to call them if Kyoko or Cydney showed their faces. I refuse to lose my family over this; next time you show up, I'm calling Chu-Chu."

He walked out leaving Reece in the room with naked women changing into their outfits. Each locker had a built in bucket that housed a single plastic rose with money in it. Each bucket was labeled Tithes and Offering.

"So you're Cydney's new goon?" a dark skin fully naked girl asked as she opened her locker.

"Yeah so break bread."

"There ain't no cup in my locker. All Black Diamond's money," she said making reference to herself, "goes home with her, sorry."

He looked at her locker door and there wasn't a star when she shut it.

"Aye, do you know why it says tithes and offerings on all these buckets?" He pointed it out to her.

"Ol' girl you work for think she's God to these foreigners and that's where the church gets its money."

She walked off with a horse's ass stuck behind her. Her black booty was so big that Reece couldn't conceal his thoughts.

"Damn, that ass fat."

She stopped walking.

"You got me fucked up. I'm not one of God's employees; you can't buy shit from me in this strip club but a dance. And I bat for the home team; you're way too handsome to have anything other than a big dick in your pants."

If the partnership worked out with Cydney, Reece would turn it into his next mission to get Black Diamond batting for his team. That was another item on his bucket list, to get a lesbian girl to go both ways if he couldn't get her to turn straight.

There was a huge locker at the end of the row that had two stars on it so he skipped over the next one to collect from it last. There were two buckets in it that both read "Disciple" and both were empty.

"Whose locker is this?" he asked to no one in particular, he just wanted an answer.

"Tomas and his goon Chu-Chu's," the women began answering at the same time.

"But it's yours now." Kyoko appeared with her shirt off behind him.

"Chu-Chu took his and Tomas' money though. I guess Tomas is still on her payroll, he mentioned something about Tomas having kids that needed to be fed to the club owner."

"Kids? Now Tomas has kids, what else didn't that bastard tell me?" Cydney asked.

Cydney had unknowingly stepped in the room behind Kyoko and at her words, Kyoko jumped."

"I paid Bossman and told him what happened. I have to go back and dance." Fear was in her words and her facial expression.

"What in the fuck do you mean you paid Bossman?"

Reece closed the locker door and smiled at Cydney.

"I thought I'd get a bird's eyes view on my investment."

He had a stack of money on his lap and when she saw it, she was pissed. She clapped her hands twice and the room cleared out. Kyoko tried to make a run for it but was snatched up by the arm.

"You stay," Cydney said freeing her from her grasp. "Reece, there is a method to collecting the money. You don't just grab the cash out of the pot. Give me the keys and let me show you."

Holding her anger in was becoming impossible. She was almost positive that Reece's move had just cost her some money.

"Did you collect from the all the lockers?" she asked taking the keys.

"All but that one right there," he said nodding his head to a locker, three lockers away from him. Cydney opened it and showed him the inside of the door.

"The owner, Miguel, puts a star on the calendar for the days they worked. I tried to have Tomas collect daily but when he couldn't, we had the calendar that we could check to see how much was owned. You see how Friday through today is marked? That means Bubbly owes me twelve hundred dollars. Now there might only be ten in her bucket because it's Wednesday and the other $200.00 isn't due until she's done dancing." Cydney reached for the money in the bucket but it was empty.

"Kyoko, is that bitch here?"

She nodded her head yes.

Cydney turned on her feet and exited the room with Reece and Kyoko following her. She searched the VIP rooms, the main floor, and then the restrooms, employee and guest. Bubbly had left the building. Cydney scanned the floor until she found who she was looking for at the bar talking and sipping on a drink. She waited until Black Diamond turned her cup up to her lips and drank before she grabbed her by her thyroid gland like she had previously done to Kyoko.

"Where's your bitch with my money?" Cydney knew she wouldn't be able to respond with her fingers in her throat, but she wanted to make sure her words were clear so the answer she received would be. When Black Diamond's eyes began to bat, Cydney let her go.

"I fucked her Cydney, that don't make her my bitch, but she did say something about going home. I think she said her stomach hurt, I don't know." She held her neck as she hit Cydney with a Kanye shrug. She continued to entertain the man she had been talking to like Cydney hadn't almost taken her life.

"Kyoko, you stay here until close. If the bitch comes back, call me. I'll get in your ass later about forwarding me to voicemail for the last four days. Reece, let's go."

"No, I come with you now. We should talk and um...catch up," Kyoko said looking over her shoulder hoping to see Brass but to no avail.

"Do what she said Kyoko, don't make me enforce it," Reece said as he flashed his gun handle at her. Cydney grinned enjoying his words.

"I'm not going anywhere, Bossman. I just thought y'all wanted to get caught up. Here..." She handed him the other $200.00 she owed. "I don't want them problems. I'll call if she comes."

******

Cydney jumped in the driver's seat and hit the gas before Reece could buckle his seatbelt.

"What time is it?"

She had a watch on her wrist but Reece went ahead and answered.

"5:45."

Instantly, she made a U-turn and a right turn and got on the interstate. Reece wanted to talk but Cydney was in a full conversation by herself and he didn't want to interrupt.

"I got something for your ass, Bubbly. When God is done with you, you will wish you were back in Belize!"

She exited the interstate and pulled into a daycare.

"Right on time! Hand me the pepper spray in the glove compartment."

Reece didn't move fast enough so she grabbed it herself and popped the trunk. He couldn't see what she was doing, but when she closed the trunk, she had a plastic trash bag in her hand.

"Bring your gun and come on," she shouted

He caught up to her at the entrance to the daycare center.

"Look, I don't know what you got planned, but I'm not shooting nobody at no damn daycare center. Like I said, I'm not your muscle."

She ignored him and entered the daycare with a huge smile on her face.

"Look at auntie's baby, come here Keith!"

Cydney snatched the three-year-old up into her arms before his mother, Benita, also known as Bubbly, had the chance to. Reece couldn't tell how Bubbly was feeling before they had walked in, but the look on her face read scared shitless.

"How was my nephew today ladies, did he have a good day?" She covered the little boy's face in kisses as the daycare workers praised the little boy for all his educational achievements at two years old.

"Ms. Adore, give me my baby back," Bubbly whispered.

Cydney didn't say a word. She let the daggers in her eyes speak her words for her.

"Thanks ladies, for all you do. You're doing an excellent job with my nephew. Say bye-bye, Keith."

"Bye-bye," baby Keith said as he pumped his hand in and out of a fist.

Cydney exited the center and made it to her car with a weeping Bubbly at her heels.

"Please give me my baby back."

"When I get my money, you can have your brat back. He's useless to me."

"I paid my tithes, they are in my locker. Please, just give me my baby back."

"It's in your locker where? And why did you leave work early, did you make my money before you left?" She put the baby down and grabbed him by his hand.

"The daycare said he had an upset tummy as soon as I got there. I didn't get a chance to dance and your money is where I always put it, in the collection tray. Come here, Keith, come to Mommy."

Bubbly got on her knees and opened her arms wide to lure her son to her but the grip Cydney had on him wouldn't allow him to budge.

"The tray is empty just like your words, Benita. You're the only immigrant turned citizen that's still on my payroll. You've been working for me since my starting days in New York. I know you're in school and stripping fits your schedule, but what I'm trying to figure out is why you have..." Cydney's eyes locked on the little boy's handsome face. "...been putting up with my shit for almost four years, unnecessarily? You don't need me anymore, especially since Tomas is dead, huh?"

Reece didn't have a clue what Cydney was talking about but he wouldn't have to guess.

"This little bastard is Tomas' son, isn't he? He brought you to Arizona so y'all could play house behind my fucking back. So what happened, Bubbly, did big cousin Chu-Chu tell you to stop working for me and you'll get Tomas' cut?" Benita slowly shook her head no.

"Don't you dare lie to God when you know that I know everything, come here little bitch!" She grabbed baby Keith by his face as she took the plastic bag out of her purse and put it over the boy's body. The bag was longer in height than he was and all that was left in view were his feet. She pulled out the pepper spray, shook the can, and sprayed it under the bag. The baby began to gag instantly.

"Man, what the fuck?" Reece yelled at her and snatched the bag off of Keith. The little boy began to scream and cry as he rubbed his eyes and threw up. The harder he rubbed his eyes the deeper the pepper spray penetrated them. Unknown to the adults around him at the time, baby Keith was now blind in his left eye. He couldn't tell them because the projectile vomiting wouldn't allow him to catch his breath and formulate already limited words. Reece grabbed him by both arms and held them over his head, but the pepper had mixed with the air and caused Reece to join in on the coughing and gagging.

"If you want to see little Tomas alive you have an hour to get my money," Cydney said as she tried to free the boy from Reece.

Bubbly was in tears and wanted to comfort her son but she knew Cydney would kill him if she got closer to him.

"Tomas loved you and you constantly took advantage of it. How long did you think you could call him partner but force him to live in that nasty motel with us in Harlem? You only gave him sex when you wanted it and laughed at his needs. Yes, we became one sexually and Keith is the product of it, but if you hadn't stabbed him in the back, this would have never happened. You think he didn't know what you did to your last partner? Or should I say fiancée?"

"SHUT UP!" Cydney screamed as she snatched the gun from Reece's waistband and pointed it from Bubbly to her son. "I want my money in an hour or you and your desperation seed are dead!"

"My car, take my car. I'll sign it over to you now."

Bubbly's Altima was far from being a lemon but the car wasn't Cydney's cup of tea. She agreed to take it with the thought of selling it for more than what was owed to her. Once the paperwork was done, she got back in her car and started it.

"You drive my car and I'll take the bucket."

Reece was against every move he watched Cydney make but there was a business transaction being made so he walked to the driver side and looked at the tear-filled mother nurturing her son.

"I'll meet you at your house after I drop them off."

"That ho had a baby by my man, let her and her raggedy ass child walk."

Blood began to drip from the baby's nose and although the vomiting had stopped, he was still having trouble breathing.

"Your man or your dead business partner? Is this shit business or personal?" Reece asked taking his gun back from her.

"Business," she mumbled.

"Okay then, we'll drop her off together since she held up her end on the business side by giving up the car."

"Whatever you say partner!" she said rolling her eyes. "I'll call Chu-Chu and have him pick the car up and…"

"Fuck those feelings you're stuck in. They have you not thinking right," Reece said cutting her off in mid-sentence. "How are you going to tell Chu-Chu the reason he needs to pick up the car is because you're taking his blood cousin who just lost his father to the ER after you pepper sprayed him? And even if he wasn't Tomas' son, the owner at the club said Chu-Chu wants you and Kyoko dead. Whatever agreement y'all made is dead."

"What the fuck happened? I delivered and Kyoko even killed Brass for him."

"That's the thing; something ain't right about that story either. Kyoko is like 100 lbs. You really think she took down a 240 lb. killer?"

Cydney had tuned him out. She needed answers and Kyoko had them. She dialed her number and got no answer. She called the club and they said she had left ten minutes after they had. Reece was right, something was up with Kyoko, but neither party knew exactly what it was.

Home Depot

"Where were you? All three of them were inside!" Kyoko exclaimed as she hopped into the passenger seat of the rental. Brass glanced around to see if anyone saw them and then pulled off. "That was your perfect chance to get at Chu-Chu, Cydney, and that bitch nigga Reece!" Kyoko pouted and tugged at her seatbelt.

"That's not how I want to do it. That fool Chu-Chu gotta pay for what he did to my mans. It can't be quick. I need him to pay slow and brutal, like a fucking college loan, you feel me?" Brass said as he looked at her. A cigarette dangled from his lips as an ash floated to his dingy tank top. He was sweating like a politician on a lie detector. The Arizona heat wasn't as welcoming as it was the first time around; or maybe his perspiration was from his nerves being entangled in anxiety- the stakes were higher this time. "Can't kill him in a fucking club. That's stupid."

"Didn't stop you before. Remember? That's how we all got into this mess to begin with," Kyoko said as she pulled down the visor and adjusted her wild hair.

"That was different. That was business. This is beyond personal." Kyoko sucked her teeth and rolled her eyes animatedly.

"Well you could've at least killed Cydney or Reece. That would've eliminated two-thirds of our problems." Brass shot her a puzzled look.

"I ain't studd'n no damn Reece and Cydney. Fuck them! I want Chu-Chu. He is the reason my man is dead!" Brass punched the dashboard and looked away out of frustration.

"You stupid as fuck, nigga!" Kyoko blurted. Brass slammed on the brakes and the car slid to the side of the road. As her head jerked forward, Brass grabbed her by her chin like an embarrassed mother in church.

"The fuck I tell you about calling me that shit! You ain't black, bitch! No matter how bad you want to be!" He forcefully shoved her face away and tried to gather his cool.

"Oh so now you gangsta?" Kyoko mumbled as she massaged her jaw. "I'll call you whatever the fuck I want to call you...nigga." Brass looked at her with eyes of rage. "You ain't been through shit! Not like me. Not like me, nigga!"

Brass wanted to smack the chitterlings out of her, but when he saw the dark sorrow in her pupils, and the tears that gathered in the tiny slits of her eyes, he knew that she was speaking from a troubled place that his imagination couldn't even fathom.

"You don't know shit…you have no idea what she is capable of…" Kyoko shook her head and looked out the window so that her nude tears could drop in privacy. "You blame Chu-Chu for the death of your friend…" she started to chuckle.

"The fuck is funny?"

She turned towards him still chuckling madly.

"You know how many friends I've lost cause of that bitch?"

"Who?" A van zoomed by causing the car to shake, and breaking Brass' thought for a second. "'Cause of Chu-Chu?"

"No, nigga! 'Cause of that bitch Cydney!" She wiped her eyes and sniffed snot through her nostrils like a nervous coke addict. "Who do you think ordered the hit on your friend, and you? Chu-Chu don't run shit, my nigga! She gave y'all up. That was the whole point of going there, and she would've gave up your boy Reece too if he didn't prove useful."

Brass just listened and let her words soak in. He had the look on his face that a child would make if you revealed the authenticity of Santa Claus too early. Kyoko noticed the look.

"Yeah, your boss and all them…that was because of her. All to keep her business afloat. A business that she now shares with Reece." Kyoko smiled, knowing that she had Brass' attention now.

"That nigga, Reece was in on it? Why are you just now telling me this?"

"I told you before, but you weren't ready to listen." Brass shook his head and punched the steering wheel as he yelled out. All of his hatred for Reece had boiled back up his throat, and he regurgitated it back into reality.

"I swear to God this nigga dead! All of them! Greedy muhterfucker. Unc was about to go legit with him, all he had to do was wait. Nah, he got greedy and had my people killed. All under the influence of that bitch!"

Kyoko was now cleaning her nails with a toothpick.

"Pussy-a-do-it…"

"How do I find them?" Brass turned towards her with red eyes.

"Shit, I dunno about Chu-Chu. He's looking for her too."

"What about her? Where is she? Where does she do business?"

"She wouldn't dare go back to her main office, but…" She looked at him and shook her head. "Never mind…"

"What? Tell me dammit!"

"Where do you think she gets the women for these establishments?" Kyoko gave him a serious look. "In front of a Home Depot?"

"I dunno…shit, fuck the riddles. Tell me where she might be."

Kyoko smiled.

"I'll do better than that, nigga. I'll show you." She giggled and pointed at him. "I'll show you what modern day slavery looks like…my nigga."

*****

Reece rode in the passenger seat of Cydney's Benz as he stared out the window. He tried to convince himself that he was taking in the scenery, but deep down inside he was forcing himself to keep down the regrets that seemed to rise in his empty stomach like Patron shots. It had all happened so quickly, and he honestly thought that he was making the right choice by joining forces with the stranger, but now the butterflies in the cave of his stomach had turned to rattled bats. He had traded one evil for another…possibly a more demonic business with more victims.

"Aye, so what was that back there?" he asked, breaking the silence once they left the hospital. Cydney adjusted herself in the seat and released a sigh.

"That was business. That's all," she answered flatly.

"Business? You call pepper spraying a toddler business?" His anger seeped out of his pores like Sunday morning alcohol. "All over some business partner's baby? Is it really that serious? Or do you just like playing God?"

"Yes, I do. What is it that you think I do 'round here?" she asked as she glanced at him. She was tired of masking the ugly side of her operation. He was in too deep to turn around and go back to the sticks of NC. so it didn't matter. "I don't run a fucking salon. I run bitches, male and female! Like a pimp of some sort, you understand now?"

Reece nodded, but he didn't understand fully.

"I get that part of it, but a kid?" he spread his palms out. "Come on now. A fucking kid." He shook his head and went back to staring out the window.

"So! Who do you think these girls are? They don't sell mint cookies; they sell pussy! Where do you think they come from? In front of Home De-"

Reece cut her off with a wave of his hand. "I get it, I get it, damn! I'm saying this, if I'm going to be your partner, I need to know everything. Don't hide shit from me, like I feel like you are doing." Cydney leaned over and stared in his eyes with a serious look.

"Where do you think these girls come from?"

"It don't matter where the fuck they come from, or what their profession is. They deserve to be treated with some type of fucking respect," Reece said without looking at her, staring out the window at the desolate highway environment.

"Oh, and when a crackhead came up short, y'all just patted him on the back, kissed him on his sweaty cheek, and said that's ok young man. Bring it next time? Fuck outta here with that sanctified bullshit. You knew what it was, and you know what it is. There is no difference."

"The difference was, if we beat a fiend, he deserved it. That kid was innocent," he fired back as he pointed out the window in the direction from which they came.

"Save the preaching for Sunday, Pastor! How you gon' sit over there and judge me like you don't have a duffle bag full of dead bodies folded into swans. You telling me none of those were innocent? None of those were kids?" Reece looked at her and shook his head. "Exactly…"

They rode in silence for a bit, as the only noise in the car was from the air whistling through the crack of the window. Cydney became irritated and raised it up, but Reece defiantly lowered it all the way down, letting the warm AZ air smack some sense into him.

"I'm just saying," he started and cleared his throat. "I left that life to escape the brutal nonsense. I wanted to go legit. Remember that? Make something out of this money?"

"Nothing is legit, Reece. Not in this country. Even if you work at McDonalds, you still have victims. The fat fucks that have heart attacks…some of them are kids. Even a fucking real estate agent has victims. She lures poor broke people into 30-year mortgages that they will die paying…this is no different. At least these girls are free after their debt is paid."

"Free?" Reece glanced at her confused. "Debt?" She shook her head at how slow he was.

"You country boys really are stupid, I see."

"Where are these girls from, Cydney?" Reece asked sternly.

"Everywhere…they are here chasing the American dream that I supply…at a cost."

"And who supplies the girls?" Cydney looked at him and smiled with a slight chuckle. "I'm not joking," he said, "I need to know what I'm getting into."

"Be real, when you were selling dope did you need to know where the coke came from? Did you ask to see the workers? The child labor that's involved? The young women that swallow balloons and die to get that shit into the country? Did you ask to see that? Do you have a swan for all of them? Nah! 'Cause if you did you'd have your wish by now…'" Cydney laughed to herself as she gripped the wheel with one hand and rubbed her face. "A fucking wish…this nigga here." She shook her head and then mocked him. "I need to know what I'm getting into…You know what Reece? I'm starting think you're not built for this shit."

Reece didn't appreciate how she was handling him. "First of all, don't come at me like I'm a bitch nigga."

"Then stop acting like one! Fuck!" Cydney slowed down and hit a U-turn. "You know what; I'll show your ass. You think you ready for this shit, then let's go meet the man."

"The man?" Reece asked as he gripped the handle as she wildly whipped the car around.

"Yeah, I'ma introduce you. Plus we gotta relocate to New York."

Reece's mouth dropped. "New York? The fuck for?"

"'Cause my shit too hot here. Chu-Chu after me over that Brass shit, so that means your boy is still alive. That's too many enemies too close to me. And you should be worried too."

"I'm not worried about Brass," Reece said as he checked his hip to adjust his pistol. "New York though…That's a big move."

"Fool, you came all the way here," she said in laughter. She straightened her face up when she saw that he missed the humor. "Listen, if you are scared, just tell me and I'll dropped you off at the house. You can get your little birds and fly back to the sticks. Just say the word..." Reece looked at her with a hard stare. He knew she was playing him, but his ego forced him to fall for it. "Let me know, country boy."

"Who is this man?" Reece simply replied. She smiled at him and sped up the vehicle.

"I'll show you..."

*****

"Don't travel so fucking close!" Chu-Chu barked. Times like that he missed his late partner Tonto. He was an idiot, but he could drive. The skinny henchmen straightened up his act behind the wheel of the van, dodging a slap from Chu-Chu. The back cargo area was packed with eight more henchmen, all holding AK's and M-4's, ready to put in work for the Mexican Mafia to earn their '13' tats. "Bitch think that she can con me and get away with it. That's a no-go!" Chu-Chu said as he looked over the Tech-9 in his lap. When he glanced up, he noticed that they were drifting over the center lane.

"Aye!" Chu-Chu slapped the driver in the chest. "Straighten this bitch up!"

"Sorry, I was trying not to hit that car that was parked on the side of the road..."

"Fuck that car. I got enemies to kill!" Chu-Chu sat forward and squinted out the window. "Where did they go? Did they turn around?" He couldn't see since the van didn't have side windows. "You lost them!"

"You told me to back off, Holmes..." Chu-Chu slapped him again, this time in the face.

"Incompetent puto!" Chu-Chu's chest heaved as he tried to calm down. "Ok, ok. We are going for the head of the snake then. This bitch knows that I'm after her now, so she wouldn't dare go home. If she is sm-"

"Where you think she going?" the driver interrupted.

"Shut the fuck up and let me finish, damn!" Chu-Chu threatened him with a fist. "Like I was saying. If she was smart she'd skip town again, but not before she hit the depot to check out."

"Home Depot?" the driver asked.

Chu-Chu closed his eyes and tried his best to find tranquility.

"Cholo, if you don't shut that stupid fucking mouth of yours, I swear before the holy Mary and her cherry, I'ma bust yo' ass!" he lunged at him but the driver flinched and nearly swerved off the road. "Now turn this bitch around."

*****

After nearly an hour of driving through the desert, Cydney turned into what seemed to be an abandoned city, packed with old buildings that hadn't seen life since the 60's. Reece's eyes stayed on a swivel as they cruised through the ghost town and eventually approached a gated complex in the rear. Two armed guards stood at the entrance of what looked like a prison almost, secluded by barbwire.

"What is this? A concentration camp?" Reece asked as Cydney reduced her speed and stopped in front of the entrance.

"Something like it," she said as she lowered the window. One of the guards, a stout hard faced character, marched to her window with his finger on the trigger of his rifle-just in case.

"What do you need?" he asked in a thick Russian accent. His cold eyes bounced from her to Reece and then to the backseat.

"Tell Bobbi Omni that Cydney is here to speak to him," she said, lacing her words with more confidence than she actually had. The guard stared at her for a second and then marched back to his partner. They called it in over a handheld radio and waited for orders. Once they heard back from the boss, the guard marched back to the car and looked them over once more.

"Follow me," he said as his partner opened the gate. The guard walked down the long stretch of gravel foundation as Cydney cruised behind him, careful not hit heels with the car like a child trailing his mother in a grocery store.

"Stash that pistol," she whispered to Reece. He felt uneasy about going in unarmed, but he was almost certain that the guard was going to check them once they parked anyway. He pulled the weapon from his waist and slid it under the seat…his nervous fingers caused the pistol to slide too far and he was almost sure that it made it to the backseat, but he didn't have time to fix that issue at the moment. The guard directed them to park next to a large warehouse, and walked over to Reece's side of the vehicle. Armed guards were scattered across the compound making patrols. They all had hard faces, cliché of Russian villains.

They stepped out and the guard approached Reece with his rifle slung on his back. He immediately started patting him down for weapons, and then gave him a suspicious look into his eyes. He then checked Cydney as well. Once satisfied he led them inside the warehouse, which seemed innocent on the outside, but that, was an illusion.

When Reece stepped inside, his eyes nearly melted from their sockets. Aligned on the walls were cages, used in zoos to house large animals, but the prized catch there were women. Five to a unit, dressed in nothing but a beige bra and panties, they all stared at the new face, and scowled at Cydney. Like stray dogs in a shelter, waiting to get adopted before the state allotted time elapsed; they watched the visitors walk by with puppy eyes from their kennels.

Reece's heart was heavy. He'd seen crackheads destroy their lives over dope, but nothing compared to seeing the immigrant women, who were once beautiful, now covered in smut with matted hair and caged like songbirds that had long ago lost their voice.

The guard led them up the stairs and to a large door. He knocked three times and a voice shouted from the other side.

"Enter!"

They followed their escort inside the room, where a tall broad shouldered middle-aged man sat behind a desk- His desk resembled Unc's, and Reece had to think about how far he had come, or how deep he had sunk...

"Why are you here?" he asked in a cliché drawl without looking up from the paperwork on his desk.

The guard stood to the side and waited patiently like a sentry.

"Um, I wanted to tell you that I have to move to New York..." Cydney spoke nervously. She had been there before, but only with an invite, and that was to take her pick of the litter. Coming unannounced just gave her a bad vibe.

"This isn't the post office of some sort. I don't require a two weeks' notice," he said as he looked over the rim of his glasses. His gray eyes shifted to Reece. "And who is this?" he asked calmly. Reece forced himself to look out of the large window that was positioned behind the man's desk, in attempts to break the cold stare.

"This is Reece, my new partner. He wanted to see the business that he was investing in. We are going to move my operation to New York. Hopefully you and I...and him...can still do business," Cydney said as she folded her hands in the front of her. Bobbi removed his glasses and leaned back in the leather chair.

"A potential business partner. And you bring him here?" he asked, and she nodded. "Let me ask you something, woman. Are you out of you fucking mind?" he snapped and he shot up to his feet- even the guard flinched. "You bring this suspect looking prick here! HERE! What do you think this is? A fucking museum?" His 6'7" frame stepped around the desk and in her face as he looked down at her with clenched fists.

"I'm sorry, Bobbi. I'm in some shit, and time isn't on my side right now. Trust me, he's cool..." Cydney spoke softly.

"You're in some shit? Awwwweeee!" He smiled and leaned into her face- right before he backhanded her, sending her to the ground clutching her cheek. The guard immediately raised his rifle and aimed at Reece in case he felt heroic. Reece just raised his arms in the air with wide eyes as he backed up to the wall. Bobbi stood over Cydney, barking insults in his native Russian language. Finally, he stepped away and went back to his desk, forcing himself to calm down.

"Get up, bitch," he ordered as he massaged his right temple. Cydney stood to her feet and brushed off her attire like nothing had happened. Reece had to admire her strength.

The uncertainty in the room grew thicker as her cell phone rang. She planned on ignoring the call but curiosity got the best of Bobbi and he urged her to answer.

"Cydney, where are you? Are you ok?" her supervisor, Mark whispered into the phone.

"I'm awesome, Mark," she lied into the phone. "But I'm done with that office. I'll get with you tomorrow about putting my transfer in so I can return to New York, I gotta go."

"Wait!" he yelled and then went back to whispering. "The detectives came in to question you yesterday about the bruise on Ms. Stella's chest."

"What bruise?"

"They found a bruise on her but that's not all they found." He got quiet.

"Look, now isn't time to pause for suspense. What else did they find?" she said irritated.

"They said traffic cameras showed a woman getting out the back seat of Yvette's car and they are certain it was you. They came back today with an arrest warrant to charge you with her death. What the hell is going on, Cyd?"

"Nothing. I'll call you back. It's just a big misunderstanding."

"Cyd…" he lowered his voice. "They've been tailing you. They are on their way right now. Where are you?"

She ended the call, pressed the volume button on the side of her phone, and continued the conversation like it never ended.

"Oh, that's nothing Mark. Don't worry about me filing for workman's comp." She laughed. "Go ahead and start my transfer paperwork and I'll be in to sign it tomorrow, bye."

"Is everything ok?" Reece asked. He had been watching her facial expressions and her laugh didn't explain the petrified look that briefly graced her face.

"Yes, everything is fine. They are working on my transfer to New York right now."

There was no way she'd tell Reece the gig was up before it ever got off the ground. New York had become a dream in a matter of seconds. She needed to flee the country and the irony of her becoming an immigrant in a strange land almost brought her to tears. Her grandfather had always told her that blood money doesn't stay folded for long and she didn't know if she had what it takes to iron out its wrinkles.

"So New York huh?" Bobbi questioned and she nodded. He looked over at Reece who slowly lowered his arms once the guard relaxed. "And you trust this character?"

"With my life," Cydney lied.

"I was asking him..." Bobbi said, holding his glare at Reece.

"I trust her about as far as I can throw her," Reece commented. Cydney shot him a look, but Bobbi broke out into hysterical laughter as he stood to his feet.

"I like this guy!" he said as he pointed and approached Reece with his hand out. "What did she say your name was?" Reece shook his hard-calloused hands and offered a professional smile.

"Reece."

"You are from the south, correct?" Bobbi asked, detecting his drawl.

"North Carolina," Reece answered, awkwardly noticing that Bobbi was still shaking his hand.

"North Carolina..." Bobbi looked up at the ceiling in thought. "First in Flight. Home of the Wright brothers, no?" Reece nodded with a smile.

"Well actually, they were from Ohio. They just came to NC to get fly..." Reece winked with a grin, causing Bobbi to chuckle again.

"Ah, and I take it, she came to NC searching for your wisdom to get her operation off the ground too. I see, I see..." Bobbi was still shaking Reece's hand...still... "Well, look. I like you so-" His words were cut off by what sounded like gunshots. The room grew silent and shots returned from outside. The guard raised his weapon as Bobbi's smile lowered and sunk into a grimace. His grip on Reece's hand tightened.

"You dare try to ambush me?"

Uncivil War

The remaining guard at the entrance glanced back and saw his partner disappear inside the building. The merciless sun was sinking just low enough to be blocked by the surrounding buildings. He pulled out a cigarette, glanced back again, and lit it quickly. His partner was cool, but he was glad that he was gone even if it was for only a few minutes. Now he could smoke in peace without someone interrupting him and bumming a smoke.

"Mind if I bum one?"

He snapped his head around and noticed the Asian girl wobbling across the path. He squinted to make sure that the desert heat wasn't playing tricks on his eyes, but sure as day, she approached him with one hand out and the other on her pregnant stomach.

"Private area. Now scoot," he said as he lit the cigarette and took a deep draw. As the nicotine hit his lungs, he closed his eyes briefly, and when he opened them, the girl was still standing there. "Did you hear me? Get the hell out of here. And how did you find this place anyway?" he asked as if the thought just hit him. He gripped his rifle tighter as the Asian girl smiled at him.

"You don't remember me?" Kyoko asked as she batted her eyelashes.

"You got two seconds to tell me how you found this place. You are pregnant, no? No way you walked this far," he said as he raised his gun in extreme suspicion.

"So you will shoot your child?" Kyoko said as she rubbed her hump. "Yeah, I was here before, on the other side of that wire. You and you dirty partner raped me, and this is the result." He paused and looked at her as if he could remember all of the women that he raped.

"Get the fuck out of here!" he barked as he turned back towards his position, but he was met with a shiny object that collided with the bridge of his nose. He stumbled back and Brass lunged forward again with the brass knuckles, this time connecting with his temple and rendering him unconscious.

"Fuck! These Russians are tougher than I thought," Brass mumbled as he caught his breath and squatted over the guard. He searched him and found the key to the gate, and took his rifle too. He tossed the pistol that he had tucked in his waist to Kyoko. "Do you know how to use one?" he asked as she examined it. She took the pillow wrapped in a hoody from under shirt, rolled it up, and pressed the wad of clothing against the guard's face. Then she jammed the pistol against the pillow and squeezed the trigger. Clothing that was once used as a pregnancy disguise, was now used as a silencer to take a life.

Brass watched in shock as she stood up straight and spat on the body. Her eyes lifted to him and her normal charisma had vanished.

"That wasn't a lie…" Brass nodded and grabbed her arm. There were a few guards on foot patrol throughout the complex, so Brass and Kyoko took cover behind a shed they found near the edge of the complex. Brass had to thank God that it was getting dark. He had no idea what he was up against, but he didn't plan on leaving until Unc and Wink's deaths were leveled.

"Now what?" Kyoko whispered. A guard was making his way toward their location and was about 20 yards out.

"We finish what they started," Brass said as he peeked out. They were running out of time. He knew if he shot the guard, then the whole complex would be alarmed.

"Promise me something." Brass gave her a weird look. "When this is done, we have to free those girls in there," Kyoko said. Brass peeked again and the guard was still coming.

"So you are the Asian Harriet Tubman, huh?" He smiled, using hilarity to mask his nerves.

"Shut up, nig-" her words were cut off by a van bursting through the gate and speeding down the gravel path. It slammed on its brakes and slid sideways as men piled out of the side door like Mexicans…then the gunfire inaugurated.

"I think it's time for us to go," Kyoko announced as she folded a piece of gum on her tongue. "That's Chu-Chu and his goons. It's about to be a bloody night once those Russians and Mexicans shoot it out. Game over Brass, you lose."

Kyoko popped her gum and then raised her gun to the back of his head but he had already taken off running towards the commotion.

"Guess I'll catch you later," she said making her way in the opposite direction.

*****

Chu-Chu stayed low in the backseat as his workers went to clear the way for his grand entrance. He could hear the powerful sound of machine guns moving farther away from him. As he sat up to make his exit from the van, Brass ran past him to get inside the building and the letters on his knuckles told Chu-Chu he had finally found his mark.

"You're dead now, pinche myate!" he said calling Brass the fucking nigga he thought him to be.

The first room he entered was empty besides three dead bodies, one belonging to a cholo he had brought with him. His follower had been shot multiple times from the stomach up causing his body to resemble a bloody and empty connect four board.

Chu-Chu pulled his diamond encrusted Rosary from its hidden spot under the neck ring of his t-shirt. He was a practicing Catholic and wore it in devotion to Mary, the virgin birth mother of Jesus. Catholic theology says that Mary made 15 promises regarding the recitation of the Rosary. Many of which dealt with the protection or sanctification of the souls of the dead. He knew the prayer by heart due to reciting it frequently. He ended his prayer by touching his forehead and saying,

"In the name of the father…" he touched the center of his chest, "and of the son," he then made the straight line into a cross on his body as he finished with, "and of the holy spirit, Amen."

The religious moment didn't last long as the thoughts of murdering everyone who hadn't come with him returned with vengeance.

******

Gunshots were getting closer to Cydney and Reece as they laid flat on their stomachs with guns pointed at them.

"Lock the doors!" Bobbi yelled to his worker as he spoke into the P.A system. "Did you think you could come in here and shoot up my establishment? I have the girl. If you want her back alive, you have three minutes to get the fuck out of here. Your time begins now!"

He flung the microphone to the floor at Cydney. His guard stopped in his tracks at the sight in front of him.

"Tell your people to leave now or you die!" he added with a kick to her rib cage.

"Those are not my people," she moaned

"Then who the fuck are they?"

Just then, the sound of sirens filled the air as a convoy of police vehicles swarmed the compound. Gunfire lit up the night sky as the Russians traded shots with the Mexicans, who traded shots with the cops. Bodies were strewn all over the area, making the place resemble Reece's first guess- a concentration camp.

Bobbi pulled his pistol and ran to the door with his guard. Reece and Cydney were lying face to face and he knew that their time was short. He whispered to her while Bobbi and the site of World War 3 distracted him and his henchmen.

"Follow me..." He hopped up, dashed behind the desk, grabbed the heavy leather chair, and slung it through the large window. The glass shattered as he reached for Cydney's hand. Shards of glass were in their palm as they tightened their grasp, bleeding into each other like a childish finger prick bond.

Bobbi turned around and fired his weapon just as Reece and Cydney made their way out the window and onto the wobbly fire escape. Bobbi commanded his henchman to go after them but when he looked over at him, he saw a trail of blood leak from the side of his mouth. The man dropped his rifle and fell forward, revealing three shots in his back. Bobbi didn't have time to react before two Mexicans rushed him inside with pistols aimed at his face. They were clearly agitated by seeing the Hispanic women among the prisoners. Without a word, they opened his body up with bullets and sent him on his way to final judgment.

~

Reece and Cydney stood on the fire escape, gripping the cold railing as they looked down. Bullets ricocheted everywhere, and they knew that their best escape route was on the roof of the warehouse. Suddenly the railing couldn't support their combined weight anymore and the structure shifted. It was hanging on by the mercy of a bolt, and their time was dwindling before falling three stories to their death.

"Come on!" Reece said as he crawled to the top. The gap to the roof was expanding so he grabbed her and lifted her up. With all of his strength, he slung her upwards and her stomach hit the edge of the roof. She started sliding down, but finally pulled herself up to stand on her feet. She looked down and saw Reece extending his hand out to her.

"Pull me up!" he said as the railing shifted again. She gave him a demonic grin and kneeled towards his awaiting hand.

"You said you trusted me as far as you good throw me...how ironic..." Reece's jaw dropped as he watched her run away. He didn't have time to experience the betrayal before the fire escape broke free of the bolt and he plummeted to the ground.

~

Brass made it through the gunfire and dashed into an empty room to catch his breath. It was mayhem all around him, so the quiet room felt a bit odd. He examined his pistol and noticed a door that led outside. He was out of ammo and knew that it was time to retreat. Hopefully everyone would kill each other and the deed would be done. He couldn't risk getting caught up in the aftermath and going to an Arizona prison, so he kicked open the door.

As soon as he stepped outside, he felt an object press against the back of his head.

"Greetings, cholo..." Chu-Chu whispered. Brass knew that it was over and didn't resist as Chu-Chu disarmed him and tossed his pistol to the side. "I'll make this quick, since I'm in a bit of a rush," Chu-Chu said as he pushed him and forced him to face him. Chu-Chu gripped the pistol with malice as he licked his lips. "This is for Tonto."

Brass was about to take off running and risk the shot in the back, but something happened, causing him to wink at his captor.

"No, this is for Wink," Brass said. Just then, Reece appeared from the side, holding the gun that Chu-Chu took from Brass. He placed it to his head and smiled at him as he squeezed the trigger...but nothing happened. Brass remembered that he was out of bullets so he sprinted and tackled Chu-Chu before he could react. They tussled on the ground for the gun as Reece stood back and watched confused. He wanted to jump in, but he was on his last leg after the fall, literally. He knew that he had to do something. He had fucked Brass over and left him for dead, all in the hopes of leaving the lifestyle behind and going legit. Now he was in an even denser shit storm.

Brass held Chu-Chu's wrist and hand, trying to pry the gun from his vice grip. The gun was slowly turning on Brass as he was being over powered. Right when Brass met the opening of the barrel, he closed his eyes and felt something heavy land on him right before the blast. He thought he was shot, but when he opened his eyes, he saw Reece's body on top of him. He had absorbed the bullet for his old partner. Brass wasted no time as he hopped to his knees, punched Chu-Chu, and took the gun from him. He slid for the gun as Chu-Chu struggled to get Reece's leaking body off of him. Even after being shot, Reece was still tussling with Chu-Chu trying to buy Brass some time- with his life.

Reece was on top of Chu-Chu, pinning him down. Brass couldn't get a clear shot, and time was running dry. He looked up and saw a group of Mexicans running their way.

"Do it!" Reece shouted as spit and blood flew from his mouth. "Shoot!" Brass hesitated but fired two shots. The first went through Reece's shoulder and struck the ground beside Chu-Chu's head. The second ripped the side of Reece's neck off and embedded in the center of Chu-Chu's head.

Reece rolled over, clutching his wound as he stared up at the stars in the clear sky. Brass stood over him feeling indifferent about the whole situation. He had come there wishing death on all of them, but after witnessing Reece sacrifice his life for him, he viewed him differently. Reece reached inside his pocket and pulled out something. He handed it to Brass as he opened his palm. It was a $100 bill folded into a crane, covered in Reece's blood.

With his last breath, as the coming group of Mexicans started shooting, he said.

"Blood money don't fold..."

Seeing Reece go out like a hero cowboy in an old western movie awoke the competitor spirit in Brass. He had to go out on a larger scale. Since he wasn't a fan of Western movies, he thought of Cleo in *Set it Off* and Tony in *Scarface* and took out as many approaching Mexicans as he could while they filled his body with more holes than you'd find in a dozen donuts. His last words if they would have been heard by anyone who cared were,

"Brass, bitch!" as he held his knuckles in front of him like a closed caption.

Cydney slid off the roof and down the fire escape on the opposite side of the building. Most of the chaos was still going on out back, so she had a clear run for the road. Just when she thought she was home free, a cop noticed her and turned his gun on her.

"Hands up!" he shouted. She was about to surrender until a cargo van pulled in between them and kick up a cloud of dust.

"Bitch, get in!" Kyoko shouted.

Cydney smiled, hopped inside, and they peeled off like a scab. Once they were free from the area, Cydney released a heavy sigh of relief.

"I knew you'd come through!" she shouted as she took off her bloody shirt and sat in her bra. The air hit her sweaty skin and she felt like she had just taken ecstasy. She closed her eyes and reflected. "Girl, we gotta leave the country. How do you feel about Italy?" she asked. She opened her eyes when she felt the van stop. She looked around and saw Kyoko smiling at her as she handed her something. She opened her palm and accepted it. It was a crane...folded out of a $2 bill...

"With ya fake ass!" Kyoko said as she punched her. Before Cydney could defend herself, Kyoko had grabbed her and pushed her to the back of the van. Cydney hit the floor and looked up. She was surrounded by women...the same women that she had made a living out of exploiting and thrown back when they no longer served her purpose. They looked at her as they all pulled out makeshift knives from the broken glass at the compound and stalked over her body like her flesh would be their last supper.

"Kyoko! Stop this! We can...we can go into business together! I got money! We can do whatever you like! Kyoko! Why?" The girls pounced on her and began stabbing her like thirsty children opening a Capri Sun on a summer day.

Kyoko just smiled as she flopped back into the driver's seat. She adjusted the mirror and popped her gum.

"Pussy-a-do-it…"

THE END